A POOR KID'S DREAM

Hell for a Hustler

Part II

A POOR KID'S DREAM

Hell for a Hustler

Part II

By: ABDUL HASAN

Copyright © 2022 by **ABDUL HASAN**

"A Poor Kid's Dream; Hell for a Hustler, Part 2" All rights reserved, including the right of reproduction in whole or in part or in any form, or by any means, electronical or mechanical.

First Edition

Cover Design by: **Kasib Hasan**

ISBN

Made in the United States of America

For information about purchases, special bulk discounts, or to provide feedback you may contact:

Twitter: **@AbdulAuthor**

Instagram: **our_way_of_life78**

(513)799-8800 or (513)383-2671

Edited by: **Ms. Lavinia Parker; P9P Ltd.©**

Dedication

This book is dedicated to the ones that fell victim to the same circumstances that I was a victim of. The victims of this street life. I know we didn't ask for this life but due to the environment we grew up in, we had to adapt to survive.

In Sha Allah you are blessed with the opportunity to think outside the box before it is too late. Change your way of thinking, then you can change your life for the better. The streets are like a vampire. They will suck your life, morality, and soul out. Many of us have become monsters, just to survive.

Knowledge of self and an awareness of a Higher Power are a must. They are the only things that can combat the devil, trust me.

For my people still in the game, it is my objective that you get something out of this book that you can use to help you through your journey.

ENJOY.

HASAN

Chapter I

Frankie was exhausted, but she knew she couldn't deny her son a good birthday party. She had just gotten off work at 6am and she slept until 12 noon, but the six hours of rest seemed like 20 minutes to her exhausted body. Her son was excited he was turning 9 years old. "Come on mama we gone be late!" Syncere said, anxious to get to the barbershop. Syncere loved going to the barbershop it reminded him of the time he spent with his father before he got locked up. "Boy you better calm down before you be going to your party with a nappy head." Frankie said, giving her son her "I mean it" stare. Syncere and his older cousin Anthony were more like brothers than cousins. Anthony was Frankie's older sister, Jamaica's son, by Greedy. Just like their fathers the two boys were inseparable. By the time Frankie pulled up on Burnet Avenue her son and nephew had her head hurting. She was relieved to have them out of her car. Standing in front of the barbershop were the regular block huggers who weren't seeing much money. Burnet Ave. used to be a heavily occupied drug infested and crime ridden block, up until Children's Hospital began buying up more and more land in the area pushing the people out. The police presence on the block was heavy which caused the hustlers to migrate to different locations in the crime filled neighborhood. Anthony knew everybody. As he walked to the entrance of the barbershop, he stopped to give everybody dap. "Boy get yo lil ass in there they don't know you!" Frankie snapped. "They do know me," Anthony responded with arrogance. At 11 years old, Anthony was too smart and too much like his father.

As soon as Frankie entered the barbershop hungry eyes fell on her. All the men were trying to shoot their shot. "Aye gorgeous." Peanut said flirtatiously. "What's up Nut?" Frankie responded, clearly not in the mood. "What up wit you? How Mell holding up? I heard they trying to give him 15." Frankie hated talking about Mell to Nut. She didn't trust any of Mell's so-called friends. "Ace how many in front of me?" Frankie asked, cutting her conversation with Nut short. "Two," Ace answered. Nut began playing with Syncere and Anthony.

Frankie used the time to get a much needed power nap in. Meechie was a well known/popular dude from Avondale. Although he was from the other side he went anywhere in the hood, whether he was getting money or just chillin' with the guys he rocked with. He had just pulled up to the barbershop seconds after Frankie walked in.

It was Frankie that made him stop his car. Meechie knew Mell was out of the picture currently and he saw this as the perfect time to shoot his shot at Frankie. He stepped coolly out of the comfort of the air conditioning in his Chevy Impala rental car and was instantly approached, "What up my nigga you need weed?" A young new jack to the block rushed him asking. "Man, naw I don't need no weed! Fuck out of here, Meechie spat, balling his face up. If a nigga want some weed he know who to ask. Stop pulling up on every nigga you see, that shit ain't cool!" Meechie said, admonishing the inexperienced hustler.

"Yo pull y'all masks down now," Squeek commanded as he stopped the stolen car in front of the barbershop. As soon as he stopped the car his two soldiers jumped out and started

shooting. Bang bang bang bang bang bang bang bloc bloc bloc

bloc bloc bloc bloc. Meechie took two bullets to the back, as

bullets shattered the windows of the barbershop. "Ohhhh my

gosh!" Frankie shrieked, when she saw her son laying on the

floor of the barbershop. Blood was oozing out of the side of his

head, she was hysterical. "Syncere!!" She began saying, in a

trancelike state. The windows of the barbershop were shot out.

Bodies were laid out on the sidewalk in front of the shop.

Several guys who were inside the barbershop when the shooting

began, who luckily were not hit, rushed from the shop before

the cops arrived.

Anthony just stood there looking down at his younger cousin

bleeding. Seeing the murder of his younger cousin would

forever change his life and his mental. A customer sat there in a

barber chair dead with his eyes wide open with a hole the size of

an egg in the side of his head. Meechie crawled on the floor

leaving a trail of blood behind him. Frankie picked her son up

with tears pouring from her eyes, as her worst fear became her reality. "Momma is here baby, don't worry you gonna be ok." She tried wiping the blood from the side of his face, but it was useless. Carrying her son outside stepping over bodies in a trance, she jumped in her car and flew up the street to the hospital, leaving her nephew behind.

***

LJ didn't know what to do, first Baby was almost killed then someone killed Low. For days he sat in his spot getting high and drinking, reminiscing. None of this was in the script they had planned. They were supposed to get rich and live it up. Now people were looking at him funny. Rumors were circulating in the hood. Some people were thinking he got Low killed in retaliation for baby. Zeek, Lows brother, had even called him from prison threatening him.

LJ was sitting in the living room at his spot in Westwood smoking a joint when his cellphone rang. "What up bruh?" He answered after seeing it was Kelvin. "Aye yo man shit just popped off on the block, three mufuckas got boxed and like four people got hit! One of em was Mell son." "What happened?!"

LJ asked in shock. "Some niggaz pulled up and just started dumping on whoever. They even shot up the barbershop! You know it was Low's people!" "Where you at bruh?" LJ asked. "I'm right here on the block." Kelvin answered. "Alright I'm bout to slide through." LJ said, already knowing who was behind the shooting. "Yo Rex, I need you to take a ride with me." Rex didn't respond with words, he simply picked his twin desert eagles up from the table and tucked them. Rex was one of LJ's young recruits. The only person besides his cousin Ghost he wasn't paranoid about being around.

LJ grabbed the keys to the Honda slider and Rex followed him out of the door of the townhouse.

When LJ and Rex pulled up on Burnet Ave. about 15 minutes later, the police were still present. He spotted Kelvin, Fred, and Slime standing in front of the building Baby used to live in on Rockdale Ave. "What up Slime?" Slime asked, greeting him. "You know Squeek and his people did this shit right?" Fred stated bitterly. "While the police up here I say we slide down to their block and say hello," Slime suggested. Fred and Kelvin were in favor of Slime's approach. LJ wasn't trying to go to war, but the war had already began. He knew he couldn't back out. There was no way they could talk this out. Low's cousin or not, Squeek had violated and there had to be repercussions for that violation. "We gon strike back but it can't be no ordinary shit! We gon hit them niggaz hard. They think they safe on that hill?! We gotta play possum, let them niggas think shit sweet," LJ commanded.

Meanwhile Downtown on 13th Hill

"We just smoked they shit up on everything!" Ray Ray celebrated the work he had just put in by buying a fifth of Grey Goose vodka and a half ounce of Kush. He was standing on 13th hill bragging to his homies. He had no remorse for the 9-year-old boy who caught a bullet to the head, or the mother of a 13-year-old boy who died after a bullet pierced her heart. It didn't matter to him that innocent people had lost their lives. Squeek was inside the building watching TV waiting for the news. Like Ray Ray, he didn't care about the innocent lives lost. All that mattered to him was getting revenge for his cousin. "Come on stupid ass nigga," Smoke said, not appreciating how Ray Ray was telling their business. Even though the few people who could hear Ray Ray were those he considered family, Smoke lived by the rule; Killaz don't talk about what they do. Ray Ray looked at Smoke and could see that he was upset so he changed topics. "Aye doe, what up with the Ritz tonight?" "You already know it's gon be jumpin." A tall, slinky, dark-complexioned kid with a mouth full of gold teeth answered. As soon as Smoke saw several cars driving down the one-way street he got on point. The same Mac-11 he had just used on Burnet Ave. laid across his stomach, under his 2x black t-shirt. As the light traffic rolled by, his trained eye looked for any signs of foul play. Seeing Smoke on point made Ray Ray wild out. "Niggaz ain't coming down here! Aye any niggaz come down here and it's his ass!" Ray Ray pulled out his twin 9mm Rugers, clutching them both so that the people in the cars riding by could see. Ray Ray wasn't worried about retaliation or the police. In his mind nobody wanted to mess with him. Squeek walked out of the apartment building and immediately saw Ray Ray showcasing his guns. "Fuck is you doing stupid ass nigga?!" Squeek barked at Ray Ray. "We don't know who these niggas is, riding slow down the block. We on deem out here!" Ray Ray said, mispronouncing the word deen, which was an Islamic word meaning you were practicing the religion. "Come on. We bout to get off the block for a minute." Squeek informed his two-man hit team. "Where we going?" Ray Ray asked. "We gon fuck wit my people up in Dayton for a minute. He been trying to get me to come up there and fuck with him anyway. He talking like he got some big plays for us." "Hell yeah, I'm definitely game to make some paper, Ray Ray responded. "Slim," Squeak called out to the tall, lanky kid with the gold teeth. "What up?" Slim answered. "You trying to get down or what?" Squeek asked, already knowing the answer. "Hell yeah!" Slim replied, eager to get in position to get some money. "Come on, we taking my truck," Squeek told them.

***

"How you feeling?"

"Man, this shit hurt like a bitch but I'm getting better. I can't wait to get back at that nigga, on errythang I'm a torture that bitch ass nigga!" Wayne stated with bitterness. Dae Dae started

chuckling. "That's what up. You already know we gon make

sure we get up wit that nigga." Dae Dae assured him. "So, Chris

gave you 30 to box Low?" Wayne asked. "Yea man, you know

Low was the only one I fucked wit foreal out of all them corny

ass niggas. But you know he chose his side, you feel me?"

Wayne just nodded his head. "I talked to your brother last

night. He called me checking up on me and shit. He asked me if

you was out here focused. I told him you was on point. That

nigga love you. All he talk about is coming home and taking

over the game," Wayne told him. "I can't wait for my brother to

come home, we really gon squeeze all these funny ass niggas

getting money out here! I'm telling you bruh, on some totally

different shit."

"All we did in there before I came home was workout, get high,

and talk about locking the city down neighborhood by

neighborhood. That nigga serious about that 'commission' shit.

He got niggaz from Columbus, Cleveland, Detroit and in the

city screaming that shit. Bruh on some mob shit forreal and

them niggaz love him." Hearing about how his brother was moving in prison made Dae Dae reflect on what he had been doing. Wayne brought him out of the trance-like state he'd drifted off to when he passed him the blunt. "Soon as I heal up we going at all them lil niggaz. Kelvin, Fred, Slime, LJ, and whoever else callin' theyself 'BG', Wayne declared with venom. "You already know. All you gotta do is heal up and errythang else a cake walk. Dae Dae hit the blunt several times then passed it back.

Chapter II

LJ stood looking down into the six-foot ditch where his little

brother would forever rest. Hot tears stung his cheeks as they

rolled down freely. Standing beside LJ was Low's mother,

Glenda. The sun beamed down on the top of the casket as it

rested at the bottom of the ditch. "You'll never be forgotten lil

bruh, I promise you. For as long as I live I'm gonna make sure

your memory lives on," LJ vowed through clenched teeth. As

Glenda stood by him, squeezing his hand, LJ said his FINAL

goodbyes. Standing directly across from them was Squeek along

with several other family members giving LJ cold stares. After

tossing a handful of dirt on top of the casket, LJ looked up and

locked eyes with Squeek. Both men shot daggers at each other

with their eyes. Two more random shootings had taken place in

Avondale since the barbershop incident and now there was a

full out Avondale and Downtown war taking place. "You ready

Mama?" LJ asked. Glenda turned around with LJ by her side

and they walked to the limousine. Glenda knew what was going on between her nephew Squeek and the guys from Avondale. As the limousine pulled out of the cemetery she reached over and grabbed LJ's hand. "I know what's goin on between you and my nephew LJ." LJ turned to face her. "Let me talk to him, I don't want my brother going through what I'm going through. He's already in prison." Glenda knew Squeek was behind the shooting at the barbershop. Although she wasn't smoking crack anymore, she was still informed on what was going on in the streets of Avondale. "Mama it's out of my hands now. Mell's relatives and several other people are after Squeek." He gave her hand a firm squeeze as she stared into his eyes. "Have you spoken to Rachelle?" Glenda asked, changing the subject. "No ma'am," LJ answered. "Well, she called me and told me she wanted to talk to you, but I didn't give her your number. I think she has some money of his. If she does, it's yours." LJ turned to the window and looked out as he felt tears building up in his eyes. Glenda knew the bond her son shared with LJ and Baby. She also knew LJ would never allow anyone to harm either one of them, let alone let them harm each other. "LJ, you remember when Baby took y'all money and lost it in the dice game and him and Low started fighting?" Glenda smiled looking back on the memory. After they had fought, she gave Low her welfare check to flip and make the money back that Baby had lost. "Yea I remember and soon as Low made the money back two weeks later Baby did the same thing again." They shared a laugh together.

"I need to go see him, I know he hurting too," Glenda told him. "I think that's a great idea," LJ told her, then instructed the driver to go to the hospital.

University Hospital

Baby laid in his hospital bed, staring up at the ceiling. Today his brother was being buried and all he could think about was the last fight they had. He wished he could rewind time. Nobody could convince him that Low was responsible for his accident, he knew Low like the back of his hand. They had fought a hundred times over the years. They were brothers nothing could come in between them. Guilt weighed heavy on his conscious. Although Low wasn't responsible for his accident Baby knew he was responsible for Low's death. Karma wasted no time coming back on him. When his aunt told him her house burned down the same day of his accident he knew why. His stash burned up with the house. Lisa had been tied up and a gun held to their daughters head the same day. Someone close to him must have thought he wasn't going to survive so they figured they'd take his stash. Only a few people knew of Lisa's house. After her apartment was burglarized, he moved her out the way and only allowed a few people to come see him there. The song "Mo money, Mo problems" that Abdul use to play all the time popped up in his head. A knock on his room door invaded the silence. Baby quickly closed his eyes. "Hello?" The door opened. Baby recognized the females voice immediately. What he couldn't understand was how she managed to visit him, and she wasn't on the visiting list that he had made out. Jazzy walked into the room and sat the vase of flowers on the windowsill. She pulled the chair up next to the bed and took a seat. I'm here Baby, like I always will be. You gotta get better because I'm pregnant, and its yours, so don't be thinking nothing stupid nigga. It was as if she could read his mind because Baby's thoughts at that moment were, "It ain't mine".

Jazzy grabbed his hand and gave it a light squeeze, "I just left Low's funeral. You need to wake up because everybody thinking you got Low killed." Jazzy had no idea that Baby was out of his coma. Only his father, his aunt Regina, LJ, and Glenda knew. He didn't want people knowing that he was conscious for a reason. Baby laid there and listened to Jazzy talk for nearly 45 minutes. She only stopped when LJ and Glenda walked in on her. Seeing Jazzy surprised LJ. Last time that he had talked to Baby he had mentioned Jazzy to him. Baby had told him specifically not to tell her he was out of his coma.

"Hey LJ, I just had to see him. I got a friend whose cousin works here. She pulled a few strings and got me in," Jazzy stated. She stood up then leaned over and kissed Baby on his lips. She then said her goodbyes to LJ and Glenda and walked out of the room. As soon as he heard the door close Baby opened his eyes. "She don't know you woke Baby?" Glenda asked. Baby just smiled. "That isn't funny boy, you shouldn't do that to her! She really loves you, I could see it in her eyes." Glenda said admonishing him. "So much going on Mama, I have to keep everybody in the dark until I can figure out what's going on. Somebody tried to kill me and since I been in here somebody tied my baby mama up and took $100k out her house. And now somebody killed my brother." Glenda looked in his eyes and saw the fighter she knew him to be. "You still ain't found my mother?" Baby knew that Laura's disappearance had most likely meant that she had relapsed. The thought of his mother back out there smoking crack hurt worse than all the physical pain he felt and there was no pill the doctor could give him to ease that pain. "Man, I'm ready to get up outta here. I need a cigarette and a joint bad as hell. Aye, you pulled down on Dae Dae yet?" Baby asked, as he raised the back of the bed up a little so he could sit up. Along with the injury to his head he had a fractured pelvis, broken leg, broken collar bone, and two cracked ribs. "Naw I ain't talked to him yet. I seen him at the funeral doe," LJ replied. "I was thinking about the argument that me and Low had. I want you to link up with Red and see if Sauce had something to do wit my accident." "I got you." "You talked to your cousin Ramon yet?" "Naw not yet but I know that money secure. I got to get up top and talk to my father's people so shit can keep rolling." Baby didn't tell LJ that he still owed Mario $375k. Neither did he mention the $140k he owed Jazzy's brother Julius. The money that his cousin had for him along with the dope he had stashed at Vivica's spot was enough for him to get back on his feet with.

His plan was to get out of the hospital, then link up with Keith and spend all the money he could put together. A few good flips and he'd have his debts squared away. After almost losing his life all he was thinking about was money. "I need you to go get up with Vivica and get that dope I got stashed at her spot and bang it for me," Baby requested. "Aight I got you. You just can't sit back for shit," LJ said with a smirk. "Shit don't stop just because a nigga get popped, you know that," Baby said with a slight smile. Glenda just shook her head. "Boy you just too much. Look at you all broken up and you still thinking about gettin' some money." "I ain't got time to sit back. Not when I got you, my daughter, my father, and everybody else to take care of," Baby said. "You ain't gotta take care of me I'll be fine," Glenda told him.

Jazzy stopped to thank her friend for getting her in to see Baby. "So how did it go?" The nurse friend asked Jazzy. "I couldn't stop crying, seeing him all messed up like that. I just wish he was conscious," Jazzy whined. "What, he was sleeping?" The nurse asked. Jazzy was confused at first. She caught on as she stood there, and when she did her temper ignited.

"You should be thankful you're still alive boy. I'm serious Antwan," Glenda said, calling him by his birth name. "I know you are, but I can't quit. I can't give up. I've been against the odds my entire life. All I know is pain, struggle, and the streets. I got to win, for Low!" Glenda knew that nothing she said would get him to change his mind. "My hood legend Magazine and DVD gon be da shit. I'm a do one dedicated to me and bruh so I can tell the real story." Knock, knock, knock. A female voice said from the other side of the door. "That's the nurse bruh unlock the door," Baby said to LJ. As soon as LJ unlocked the door Jazzy stormed inside. "Why da fuck y'all playing childish ass games with me LJ?" Baby closed his eyes, pretending to be sleep. Jazzy gave his cheek a painful pinch that caused him to yell out in pain. "Bitch what da fuck wrong with you?!" Baby snapped. "Ooh I wish you wasn't fucked up so I could fuck you up myself! Why you have me sitting here crying and pouring my damn heart out to you for a hour while you actin' like you unconscious nigga?" Jazzy yelled. "When? I don't know what you talking about girl, you trippin!" Baby lied. Jazzy gave his cheek another painful pinch. "Aww hell nah! And you laughing, whatever yo name is bitch! You about to get fired, because this crazy ass bitch don't even supposed to be in here!" Baby said to the nurse friend. Glenda tried to contain her laughter but couldn't. "As soon as you left I told him he was wrong for acting like he was still in a coma." Glenda informed Jazzy. "And you!" Jazzy turned her attention to LJ. LJ never saw the punch to the gut coming. He doubled over when the blow connected. "You been lying to me for how long LJ?" LJ responded by walking up to Baby and pinching the other side of his face. The entire room erupted in laughter, everyone besides Baby that was.

Chapter III

There were no words that could define what Mel was feeling.
Grief seized him from all sides. He no longer cared about his
fate with the federal court system. The one thing that meant the
most to him in this lifetime had been taken away from him, and
there was nothing that he could do about it. Sitting on his bunk
he smoked cigarettes back-to-back. Everything foul that he had
done on the streets came back to haunt him tenfold. The pain
that he had inflicted onto other fathers had somehow returned
back to him. Mel stood up and walked out his cell downstairs to
the phones. One phone was open, as it always was, but only
certain people were allowed to use it… until now. Mel walked to
the phone and dialed his mother's number. He could feel eyes
on him, but he didn't care. He was using the phone, and he
didn't give a fuck who didn't like it! "Aye my nigga, what you
doing?!" Face asked. Face was the pod bully. He had beaten up
several inmates since Mel had gotten there. "What up Mama,
you talked to Frankie today?" Mel asked his mother. "Yes, I

talked to her this morning," his mother answered him softly.

"Call her on three way for me." Mel responded, ignoring Face.

Face didn't like that one bit. "Aye Mel! Fuck is you doing my nigga?!" Face asked again, walking up on him. Without warning Mel cracked him with the receiver of the telephone in his mouth, he then whacked him again and again until he dropped to his knees. He continued beating him mercilessly until the guards rushed in and pulled him off him. He broke several of his teeth, and several of the bones in his face were broken due to the attack. Mel screamed he was going to kill him as the guards dragged him from the pod.

Baby sat up in his hospital bed furious. "You need to just calm down because there's nothing you can do about it now. I already spoke to my brother. He's not trippin over the money you owe him," Jazzy stated, trying to get Baby to be optimistic about his situation. "Fuck all that! One of them niggas behind Vivica and my baby mama getting tied up and robbed," he shot back. Ever since LJ had told him about Vivica's spot getting invaded, he had been in a sour mood. He knew it wasn't a coincidence that Lisa and Vivica's homes had been hit in the same day. "You telling me to calm down?! All my fuckin money is gone! My cousin done ran off and got a new number! I been in this hospital a fuckin month and everything I built done fuckin collapsed!" "Look Baby everything you lost I promise you'll get back." Jazzy said in a soothing voice.

The way that she said it was as if she was sure he would. "And how? Tell me how Jazzy?" He asked her with a sigh. "Because I'm going to help you. By the time you heal up and can move around I'll have the money waiting for you to go get it," she said. Baby stared deep into her eyes and what he saw brought a smile to his face. "So you gon get in the mud with me?" He asked her. "If that's what I have to do to help you, yes I am." She answered him. They just stared into each other eyes for a moment, as if they were communicating through them. The ringing of the hospital phone echoed through the room. "Hello?" Jazzy answered the phone. "Let me talk to Baby Jazzy." "Here, it's LJ." Jazzy said, handing him the phone. "What's up big bruh?" "You talked to China or Frankie?" LJ asked. "I'm about to call her," Baby promised. After LJ hung up Baby just stared out the window. He knew Frankie was going through it right now and Mel was even worse. Right then he knew he wouldn't be able to keep the promise that he made to Glenda. Squeek had to answer for Syncere's death. He called his cousin China's number.

"Hello?" China answered the call. Baby could hear it in her voice that she had been crying. "Aye cousin." Baby said, at a loss for words. "Baby!!" China had also been under the impression that Baby was still in a coma. "Shhh! I don't want nobody knowing I'm conscious girl, how is Frankie?" Baby responded. "I'm right here with her now." China told him. "Bring her with you and y'all come and see me. But don't tell nobody I'm woke, NOBODY, China I'm serious!" Baby commanded. "We on our way. What room you in?" China asked. "I'm a have my friend Jazzy meet you in the lobby." Jazzy gave him a cold stare after being referred to as just "a friend". "Your friend? Boy that's your girl. You always talking about you ain't messing around with her no more but errytime I look up you with her. I told yo ass you was gon meet yo match didn't I?" China shot. "Man whatever, I'll see y'all when y'all get here bye!" Baby hung up the phone. "So all I am is a friend now huh?" Jazzy said, wasting no time confronting him. "Don't start, please, I'm not in the mood. I got too much shit on my mind right now. Besides you know what you are to me. We ain't gotta put titles on it or say it." Baby tried easing her mind. Jazzy knew that was his way of saying she was his girl and that was enough for her. When China called and told him she was downstairs he sent Jazzy down to get them. While he waited, he thought about what he could do with the $33k he had on him the day of his accident and the $24k LJ had gotten from Dae Dae. He could go up top and explain to Mario what the situation was. The more he thought about it though, he didn't like the idea. He didn't want to make his father look bad. When he was able to go see Mario, he wanted to have all his money. He didn't like it when money he was owed came in portions his self. Fuck it! He said to himself.

Gotta sell the jewelry, cars, everything gotta go! His thoughts were interrupted when the room door opened. China was the first one through the threshold. Seeing his face and head she broke down crying. "Oh my god! Look at yo face, is these staples in yo head?" China said sobbing. "I'm still a pretty young fly nigga, ain't I?" He asked. "Yep!" Jazzy answered for her. "What's up Sis?" Baby turned his attention to Frankie. "How you holding up? I know there's nothing I can say to ease your pain. Just know as long as I'm breathing, I'm here for you. Even like this." He said, referring to his current physical condition. "Who did that shit? I know you know Baby." Frankie said seriously. Baby knew who was behind the shooting, but he couldn't tell her. Frankie would involve the police and that was something he couldn't play a part in. "I really don't know." He said looking her in the eyes and lying. "My son was only 9 years old. He didn't have nothing to do with whatever the fuck you mixed up in! I lost my fuckin' son, and you sitting here lying in my face! I know you know who did that shit! And I know it was one of Low's cousins!" Seeing Frankie upset almost brought tears to his eyes. He couldn't be mad at her for directing her anger and agony towards him. Truth be told he was the root of all the current problems in his life. "You better find out who the fuck killed my son you fuckin devil!" Frankie spat. China had to restrain her when she lunged towards Baby. "She needs to go!" Jazzy said, as she jumped up kicking off her sandals. "Because if she don't I'm a have to beat her muthafuckin ass!" Frankie went from 100 to 1,000! She began spitting and shouting, security had to be called to escort her from the room. "Let me get her home, I'll come back." China told Baby, as she walked towards the door. Before opening the door, she stopped and turned around. "I admire your loyalty to my cousin but you know Frankie going through a lot," she said to Jazzy. "And if you got a problem with her, you got a problem with me!" "China, I don't have a problem with you or your homegirl. I just felt like she was attacking him and I ain't going for that. Ain't no beef though." Jazzy said speaking up for herself and her man. After China and Frankie had left Baby laid in his bed thinking about what Frankie had said to him. Jazzy knew what was on his mind. "Baby don't feel bad. It wasn't your fault what happened to her son," Jazzy said trying to lift his sprit. "You say that now until it's the child in your stomach laying on a slab of metal in the morgue," Baby told her. Jazzy was at a loss for words as she thought about the child she was carrying. "I gotta do something about it. Anybody that hurts one of mine gotta answer for it," he said sternly. He thought about how Vivica made him feel when Gudda got shot and robbed.

"What about me? What about this baby I'm carrying? Who gon protect us if you gone? You gotta think about your kids. You ain't no fuckin' guardian angel or superhero!" Jazzy was so upset, she stormed out of the room before the tears could roll down her face. "Fuck dat bitch!" Baby said out loud to an empty room. He sat alone for several hours wrestling with his conscience. His mother's words came to him out of nowhere. Had he let the streets turn him into a devil? Alone, he was forced to face himself. He could lie and put on a facade to everyone else, but not to himself. He feared what lie ahead for him. Yet, at the same time he was too afraid to turn back.

Chapter IV

"You better stay out of trouble. I don't want to see you in here again you hear me?" Baby smiled at the middle-aged bald woman who had been his nurse for the past 6 weeks. She was also a very good friend of his aunt. "You won't see me in here again Ms. Marple, I promise you that." Baby assured her, meaning it. He had already made a vow to himself no more hospitals. He had enough stitches and surgeries. China and his Aunt Regina were there for his discharge. He worked out an agreement with China that he could stay at her place until he healed up, but only under three conditions. #1; No drug activity. #2; No company. #3; He had to watch her son on the days she had to work. Regina tried to talk some sense into her nephew during the ride to China's house, but it was like talking to a brick wall. He told her everything she wanted to hear but she saw it in his eyes that he wasn't finished running the streets. She knew only God could save her nephew and that there was nothing she could do or say to get him to change his ways. "I just pray God wakes you up before it's too late. I'd rather visit you in a prison than at the cemetery." Those were the last words she told him before she walked out of China's living room.

"What type of shit is that to say man?!" Baby said. "She burning bread on me." "She just telling the truth and I feel the same way. You only 16 Baby! How many times you done been almost killed?! That shit ain't normal." China yelled. "Man, that shit happens every day. I know niggas that done been shot 3 and 4 times, on different occasions. It comes with the territory," Baby said rather nonchalantly. China just shook her head at her cousin's foolish way of viewing life. Baby changed the subject, "I'm hungry as fuck too. Fix a nigga something to eat in this bitch!" "First off nigga this ain't one of yo hoes spots! Watch how you talk up in here and second of all, I ain't yo servant or maid," China snapped. "You the one said you was gon look after me," Baby refuted. China ignored him and pulled a bag of weed and several boxes of cigars from her purse and tossed them to him. Baby wasted no time putting a fat blunt in the air, shortly afterwards he was snoring out cold. China went into the kitchen and began preparing a meal for him to eat. She was almost finished when Jamaica and Frankie showed up. "Shit, his ass gon babysit Anthony too," Jamaica stated. "Girl he ain't going nowhere what else he gon do?" China said with humor. Frankie didn't do much talking. Syncere's funeral was just days ago. She was still trying to come to terms with her son being dead. She would never see him smile, hear him laugh, or tell him to stop running inside the house again.

China knew her friend was going through a rough time. She did everything she could to try to at least keep her doing something other than thinking. While China waited on her cornbread to finish cooking, she sat in the kitchen with Jamaica and Frankie. They sat there smoking weed and drinking Grey Goose. "Girl I gotta go get Anthony from school," Jamaica announced. "You might as well pick Lamar up for me," China said, hoping that she would agree. "Bitch you owe me." Jamaica said grabbing her purse, cell phone, and car keys off the table. "Bring another bottle back too," Frankie said. It's too early to be getting drunk, Jamaica thought to herself. She wanted to tell her sister, but she held her tongue. It was ten minutes 'til 3:00. "I'm about to go upstairs and take me a shower before Jamaica get back, you okay girl?" China asked Frankie. "Gone and take your shower." Frankie told her as she walked to the living room. Baby was sound asleep, snoring like a bear. Frankie noticed his prescription bottles on the table. She read through the bottle labels and saw that one of them was 30mm Percocet. She took four of the pills out and quietly placed the bottle back on the table. She had taken the strong pain pills several times before with Mel, so she knew what they were and how they made you feel. By the time China came back downstairs from her shower Frankie was feeling the effects of the addictive and powerful opioid. When China saw her smoking a cigarette she stopped and did a double take. "I know you ain't smoking no nasty ass cigarette girl?" China said, as if her eyes were playing tricks on her.

"I'm grown ain't I?" Frankie replied, enjoying the cool smoke of the Newport she had taken from Baby's pack. China was about to go in on her friend when Baby yelled out, "NO!" They both turned to see him still sleeping. China walked up to him and noticed he was sweating heavily. "Please God no! I'll do anything." Baby tried to plead for Low's life as the Grim Reaper snatched his soul. Low stared into his eyes as his body crumpled to the ground. "I'm coming back for you." The long skeleton fingered Reaper said to him. Baby pulled out his .357 and began shooting The Reaper. He just laughed an eerie, bone chilling laugh though. The face of the Reaper was a black shell with fire in its eye sockets and sharp teeth in its mouth. It was like nothing he had ever seen before, but he wasn't afraid of him. He ran to Low's body and tried reviving him but nothing he did helped. "I'm sorry bruh, I'm sorry!" For a minute China and Frankie stood over Baby listening to him talk in his sleep but when China saw tears begin to roll down his face, she woke him up. Baby woke up breathing heavy and startled. "Boy you might need to go see a doctor because you got psychiatric issues,

I'm serious." China told him. Baby fumbled with his cigarettes with shaking hands trying to light one.

After several attempts he was able to light his cigarette. "Girl look at him! He look like he seen a ghost. I'm calling Aunt Regina, you might need to go back to the hospital boy." Baby was zoned out from the dream he had just had. In his mind he had just experienced some outer body, supernatural shit. It had him spooked. He continued sweating, although he was cold. A cold he felt in his heart. "Auntie something wrong with this boy, you need to get here!" China said into her cell phone. All of a sudden, Baby began shaking. China dropped her cell phone. Frankie knew he was having a seizure. She told China to help her turn him on his side. "He gon swallow his tongue!" China said. "Girl that ain't true you can't swallow yo tongue, but you can bite it so put something in his mouth." After a few minutes he began snoring. China called 911.

Chapter V

"Bout time you reached out to a nigga. I can't believe you just

now letting me come see yo punk ass! That's crazy bruh because

I been worried about you." LJ told him sincerely. "I been going

through a lot. You know they found my cousin Ramon's body

down in West Virginia after he been missing for two months

and I still ain't seen or talked to my mama. And then, in the

midst of all that, I been going back and forth to therapy trying

to get back right," Baby explained. "Nigga you look like you

been working out and shit. You know Jazzy told me she was

pregnant with your son." LJ went on. "What's up with Lisa?"

Baby asked. "I ain't seen or talked to her?" LJ said. Baby turned

his head and took a deep puff of the blunt in his hand. "After

the robbery she packed up and moved to North Carolina,"

Baby informed him. LJ could see that it really bothered Baby.

"Do you blame her?" LJ asked. Baby turned and looked him in

the eyes. "Naw I can't blame her. I just wish I knew who did

that shit. They put a gun to my daughter's head. That shit

fucked Lisa up man. I'm on some different shit this time. I been reading books and watching documentaries on everybody. Joseph Kennedy, Larry Davis, Warren Buffet, Kenneth Supreme McGriff, Big Meech, Larry Hoover, everybody! I got some shit I'm about to put down." Baby said. LJ could see the sparkle in his eyes. Whatever he was thinking, LJ had no doubt he was going to do it. "You know I got some money saved up, so if you need to hold something to get back on your feet it's yours." "Naw I'm good. I gotta do this for myself, that way I appreciate it. A fool and money will shortly part ways. I was foolish so the money turned off on me but this time I'm a do it 10 times bigger and smarter." Baby said. Anthony and Lamar came down into the basement. "What up with you?" Anthony asked like he was talking to his peers. "Get yo bad ass upstairs boy." Baby told him. "I'm bored." Anthony said hopping onto the couch next to him and Lamar sat on the other side of him. "What y'all want?" Baby asked in a stern voice. "Let me hit the weed." Anthony said. Baby responded by putting him in a headlock. LJ stood up and began going to Anthony's body. Lamar jumped up and tried to help Anthony. "Oh you trying to help him?" LJ asked Lamar like he was serious. "Get off my cousin nigga!" Lamar said standing his ground. Lamar started swinging wildly and one of the punches caught LJ in the groin and he doubled over. What happened next shocked Baby. Lamar was only 8, so when he tried to stomp LJ out Baby started laughing, "Fuck is you doing?" LJ asked after several kicks to his body.

He grabbed Lamar and pulled him to the ground. "These little niggas is savages." LJ stated. Baby was so proud of Lamar. "Here y'all better not tell y'all mamas." Baby warned them before allowing them to hit the blunt once. Anthony went first immediately choking afterwards and Lamar was no different. LJ began reminiscing on when Zach and his boys passed them the blunt to hit for the first time. Anytime he reminisced Low was involved in the memory, and it always hurt when he thought about his brother. Baby knew what LJ was thinking once he said, "Remember when Zach did the same thing to us?" His entire demeanor changed, and Baby knew why. "We gon find out who boxed bruh and we gone torture them!" Baby vowed with venom. "That shit still fuck with me. It's like damn how could that happen?" LJ asked in a hushed tone while staring down at the floor. "Bruh I was gone get Flip, but I rather have you with me. When I went to my cousin's funeral the bitch from West Virginia he was messing with pulled my coat to what she believed happened." "What was she talking about?" LJ asked looking up from the floor no longer in his daze. He sat alert eagerly waiting for Baby to fill him in on the details. "The niggas he thought was his boys backdoored him. That's what her little brother told her." Baby said. "I guess we going to West Virginia then!" LJ replied. Charleston, West Virginia was totally different than what Baby and LJ were used to in Cincinnati. Candace, LJ's mother rented a SUV from the airport with Georgia plates and drove down there.

Ramon's female friend, Ashley (who he so happened to have 2 children by that he never mentioned) lived in a subdivision of Charleston called Cross Lanes. Ashley already had a rental for them with tinted windows and West Virginia plates so they could blend in. Ashley was biracial (black & white) She wasn't super model pretty, nor was she ugly. What was odd was she worked at the county jail in the medical ward. She lived in a modest two-story, four-bedroom home with her children and younger brother Stevie. "Y'all be safe down here." Candace said before heading back to Cincinnati. "We good mama. We'll see you when we get back." LJ promised her. "You stay out of trouble." Candace added pointing to Baby. "What I do?" He asked defensively. Candace didn't even waste her breath she just rolled up her window and pulled off. LJ followed Baby back into the house. Ashley was sitting on her couch with her 7-year-old son Ramon Jr. and her 3-year-old daughter Ramona. Ramon Jr. stared at the two strange men he had never seen before. Strange men was something they weren't used to seeing in their home. When Ramon was alive he did his business in Orchard Manor AKA the "Woo" and in Amundaville AKA the "Ville". He never brought anyone to Ashley's home, not even his crew from New York.

"Call your little brother and tell him come holla at you, don't tell him we down here." Baby told her. Ramon Jr. continued to just stare at them while sitting close to his mother. "What's up boy, I'm your cousin. Your father was my first cousin." Baby said, trying to put the kid at ease. "What's your name?" Baby asked. Ramon just continued to stare at him. While they waited for Ashley's brother to arrive Baby and LJ strapped up and put on their bullet proof vests that they had brought along for the task they committed to. Stevie wasn't what they expected. Stevie was a high yellow curly haired pretty boy. But he didn't come alone. When he saw Baby the first thing that caught his eye was the long painful looking scar traveling from his hair line down to his jaw on the left side of his face. "So, what you know about my cousin's death?" Baby asked him aggressively. LJ could read the guy with Stevie, he was the one. LJ knew a gangsta when he saw one. Stevie looked to his associate, a short, stocky, beady eyed, brown skinned dude with dreadlocks and bad acne. Then he spoke "This my boy Scooter, he was close with your cousin. Scooter the one who was out there putting in work whenever Ramon needed him to. He from City Park." Stevie said, introducing Scooter. "What up man who killed my cousin?" Baby asked Scooter directly. "I've been wondering the same thing. Only person I can see who been coming up since he got hit is Wise," Scooter said. When Baby heard the name Wise his mind flashed back to his cousin's funeral. The tall, brown skinned dude with wavy hair appeared in his mind. "That's his boy from up top ain't it." Baby asked. "Suppose to be. Since Mone been gone Wise done took over City Park using Black as his enforcer. I can't see nobody from around here hitting Mone without help from the inside because he only dealt with a few niggas and the ones he did deal with, he let eat. He was messing with a chick named Keoka from out my way. That's where niggas use to always meet him at when they copped from him," Scooter went on. "So where this Keoka bitch at?" LJ asked. "She stay on the side of the projects in a house. She dance at the strip club downtown doe," Scooter answered. "Well I guess we going to see this bitch!" Baby said. "Hold on bruh, we don't wanna jump too soon. We ghosting right now." "Aye," LJ said turning to Scooter and Stevie. "We need to know everybody Ramon was dealing with. Who he had running his spots, who he sold work to, anybody you seen him with. We need all the info you can get on them names and addresses." LJ said taking control of the situation. Ashley sat there listening, not saying a word and that bothered LJ. "We need to talk in private." LJ told Baby. They walked out to Ashley's backyard.

"Yo, we don't know how deep this shit about to get. Bodies start dropping we might have to body shorty, her brother and the lil nigga Scooter. We can't let our left hand know what the right hand doing, you feel me? Gotta be a lot of misinformation going on, you feel me?" LJ wanted Baby to know exactly what they were about to embark on. They were putting their lives and freedom on the line. "I guess we gon be here for a little while huh?" Baby asked. "You can't rush perfection. We bout to be on some real live Keyser Söze shit! However you say the mufucka name." LJ said, referring to the villain in *The Usual Suspects*. When they went back inside the house Scooter stood up from where he had been sitting and began to talk, "My nigga, I know y'all don't know me from Adam but all I got is my word and my honor. Mone was like a big brother to me since when he was just making bread down here. I'ma help y'all find out who killed him and we gon smoke they ass. Whoever was involved."

Baby and LJ could see the sincerity in his eyes but looks could

be deceiving and they both knew that firsthand.

Chapter VI

Wise sat in the apartment of a high rise located in City Park

projects. This is where he ran his operation and communicated

to his workers via chirp cell phones. City Park was just one of his

money makers. He had two more spots in Charleston that he

had workers running for him. Godson and Science were the

only two people that he always kept with him no matter what.

Both were childhood friends of his and they had been tried and

tested over the years. All three were from the Bronx, New York

and they repp'd their borough to the fullest, no matter what city

and state they were in. Wise had just started coming to West

Virginia with Ramon a little over a year ago. At first they were

just selling weed making a little money. Then Ramon came

through with the coke and heroin and that's when the money

started pouring in. Back in New York Wise was just another thug looking to come up. After losing his scholarship for basketball at Georgia Tech behind a drug and gun case he went to prison for two years. When he returned home to New York he was flat broke, unable to even buy a pair of shoes for his then 7-year-old son. The once neighborhood basketball star was just another nigga until he bumped into Ramon. Ramon told him about the move to West Virginia. With a three-man crew they sewed up the weed game in Charleston simply by keeping that fire. Wise saw three times the money he was making in college selling weed. Once Ramon's weed operation began expanding, Wise, who held the operation down when Ramon was away, began mixing and mingling with the locals on his own. He started building his own alliances. At 6'5 he was tall, broad shouldered, and handsome on the eyes to the ladies, with his New York swag. The women of West Virginia all chased him, even the ones who were already in relationships. "Yo Godson, we hittin' the strip club tonight so we need to go cop something to wear," Wise commanded. Godson, who wasn't much of a talker, just nodded his head in agreement. Science, on the other hand, was much more like Wise. He craved the attention and notoriety he received from the locals. "We gotta slide over to Huntington and check out my pretty new thang," Science announced. "Call her and tell her to have two friends ready. These West Virginia hoes freaky as hell," Wise said. While Science made the necessary phone call, Wise and Godson finished counting up the money that was neatly stacked on the coffee table. City Park was a gumbo pot located in the east of Charleston. The projects were mostly townhouses with two high rises. The Charleston Police couldn't contain the drugs and violence in the gated community. City Park sat up on a hill, the side of the projects was a row of houses and that's where Keoka lived. A 3-bedroom house with her little sister and 2 kids. At 24 years old, Keoka had a 5-year-old son and a 2-year-old daughter. Her son's father was killed before she gave birth to him, and her daughters father was a deadbeat. The only thing Keoka had going for her was a pretty face and a banging body. She was the highest earner at the strip club where she worked. She had stopped dancing regularly when she was with Ramon. Some days she cried herself to sleep when she thought about

Ramon. Ramon was a straight up thorough nigga. Unlike any other man she had ever met in Charleston. She had never been out of the city until she started messing with Ramon. "Keli!" Keoka called out to her 20-year-old sister. Moments later Keli trotted down the stairs into the living room, clearly wanting to know why her sister was screaming her name like the house was on fire. "What do yo want?!" She asked her sister, upset over the fact that she was interrupted from studying for an exam she had tomorrow. "I just got a call. I'm going in tonight, so I need you to watch Jason and Sandra," she stated. "You know I got exams tomorrow," Keli protested. "How you think you paying to take them exams?" Keoka countered. "They scheduled a last minute birthday party and you know I'm their best dancer and I gotta be there. I know you want me to keep getting this money don't you?!" Keli just turned around and stormed back up the stairs to her bedroom where she spent most of her time.

When she got back to her room, she picked up the English book she had been studying from and started back reading. Keoka went to the living room and was sitting on the couch talking on the phone when the front doorbell rang. When she got to the door and saw who it was, she told her friend that she would call her back. Black was standing on her porch with his cousin Mannie. She opened the door and Black the older cousin entered the house with Mannie right behind him. Keoka hated that she got involved with Black, but she really didn't have much of a choice. "What do y'all want?!" Keoka asked, closing her front door. Black and Mannie made themselves comfortable, taking a seat in her living room. Black propped his timberlands up on her living room table like it was his house. "You know it's my birthday right?" Black stated while lighting his Newport. "Yea and?" Keoka said, removing his feet from her table. "I want you to dance for me tonight. Call all your friends and tell 'em to slide through tonight. The singles gon be raining by the thousands. I got some people coming in from Atlanta so I wanna show them a nice time. You know ever since you put that move down for me you been acting real distant? You got me wondering if I can trust you with our secret or not... I mean your brother is my nigga and I love him like a brother..." Black said, stopping what he was about to say on purpose. "I never hung out with you or messed with you before so what you mean I'm acting distant? You got me involved in something I ain't want no parts of in the first place!" Keoka was close to tears as thoughts of what they did came to mind. "Sometimes in life you gotta do what's best for your family. Little Wan could be laying in the cemetery, then how would you feel? Just remember, he able to walk around here because of me." Black continued on. "My kids upstairs, so is that all you wanted? I'll see you tonight at the club," Keoka said, clearly frustrated. Black stood up and walked up on her until his lips were only inches from hers. "You should be nicer to me. I looked out for you, your sister, and both of your brothers. It won't hurt to give me some of that pussy here and there!" He said with an evil smirk. Keoka pushed him back. "You know if Al wasn't locked up you wouldn't be doing what you doing, so maybe you should be nicer to me!" Keoka spat. Black started laughing, "He ain't running shit out here no more. His whole circle locked up, he don't hold no weight out here! I'm the new King of the Hill, remember that." He said cockily and gave her ass a hard smack as he walked past her to the door.

***

"Damn, it's hella bad bitches in here tonight!" Science said.

They were posted up in the back of the strip club where all the action was. Strippers were everywhere, "shaking what they mamas gave 'em", the DJ was playing all the latest club bangers, and the weed smoke was heavy. The club was definitely jumping. Wise had the sour diesel burning. "Yo there go son and them," Science said, letting Wise know that Black and his people from Atlanta had finally arrived. Wise watched Black walk through shaking hands and giving niggas daps. The alliance Wise had with Black allowed him to lock up Charleston. Unlike Huntington, Charleston was full of out of towners. New York, Detroit, and Ohio mainly, but everyone was chasing money. The dope game was sweet. Dope was two to three times higher, and you could sell mediocre dope and get away with it. Black walked up to Wise, gave him dap and greeted him. "What up my nigga? This my people Rasta." "What up yo?" Wise said, sticking his hand out. Rasta was a light-skinned dude with wavy hair, and he spoke with a heavy Jamaican accent. Mannie and the rest of Black's entourage stood around like bodyguards while Black sat with Wise and Rasta discussing business. They were the heavy hitters in the club and all the dancers could see it by the clothes, diamonds, and gold that they wore. Rasta was the plug that Keoka's brother Al had turned Black on from the feds. Selling dope wasn't what Black did, he was the enforcer. Instead of trying to play a position he wasn't qualified to play he turned Rasta on to Wise. The more money Wise made the bigger cut Black made. Black oversaw the workers, and if they came up short with the money he paid them a visit. All the lil niggas that he knew that wanted to hustle, he took to Wise, and Wise gave them a pack to push.

"Damn son! Who is that right there?!" Science said pointing. Wise spotted the gorgeous red bone. She was a tall, thick, exotic work of art and she was tossing money on Keoka while Keoka danced for her. Beside her was a caramel complexioned female, not quite as good looking but for damn sure close. Wise knew that they weren't from West Virginia. He could tell by the designer purses and heels that they were wearing. These were bitches with money, or at least bitches that had been around niggaz with money he thought. "Go get 'em Science," Wise said. He didn't have to tell Science twice. He watched Science walk over to the two lovely females, then he saw the ladies both turn towards where he was and smile. Black stepped up and stood beside Wise as Science escorted the two women over. Wise automatically knew which one he wanted. "This my man Wise. This Godson. That's Black, and that's Rasta," Science said introducing the two women to his crew. "This is Sophia," Science announced, pointing to the one that Wise was interested in. "And this is Grace," Science said, waving towards the friend. "Where y'all from?" Wise asked. Sophia spoke first. "I'm from Chicago." "And I'm from Huntington," Grace said. "You drink or smoke?" Wise asked. "Sophia don't, but I do," Grace assured. Wise poured her a glass of champagne and handed her a cigar to break down. "So, where y'all from?" Sophia asked. "We gypsies baby, we ain't got no home, we rollin' stones." Wise ensured her with a smile. "That was cute." Sophia told him with a smirk. Black sent one of his flunkies to go get Keoka, seeing that Wise and Science had taken claims on Sophia and

Grace. Godson stood off to the side watching everyone in the club. He didn't talk to anyone. Unlike Wise and Science, Godson didn't wear any jewelry. It wasn't that he couldn't afford it, he just wasn't into jewelry and flossin'. While he stood watching his homies fraternize with the two women that they had just met, he wondered if the people who killed Ramon was there in the club? The Little Page crew was posted up not too far from where they were. The Saint Albans boys were in the building as well. Every hood had its ballers, but City Park was where it was at right now. And Wise held it down for City Park. Sticks, a skinny, pimple faced dude in his mid 20s had Little Page on lock. He used to rock with Ramon before he died but since Wise had taken over he linked up with Bonjo from Orchard Manor. The Saint Albans boys didn't like the fact that the New York niggaz were running through Charleston getting money. Ramon tried to link up with a few dudes out there but they declined his offer. Godson had a feeling that someone from Saint Albans was behind Ramon's murder. Ramon was a good dude in Godson's eyes, therefore he felt it was necessary that he avenge Ramon's death. Wise didn't want to disrupt his money flow with beef, but he vowed that when the time was right that they were going to bring sweet justice to the person (or persons) who killed their friend. Two dancers walked up on Godson and began twerking on him. "I'm good," he told them. "Your friend gave us $500 dollars to come keep you company," one of the dancers responded. Godson looked up to see Black smiling at him, while Keoka was bent over making her ass bounce all over his crotch. "No disrespect to y'all beautiful Earths, but this ain't my thing Queen." The dancers were taken aback. They looked at each other, then back at him. One of them spoke up. "You're different, but I like that sweetie. A bitch gotta pay her bills and feed her kids tho'." "A bitch is a dog. You're not a dog, you're a black woman. Mother of civilization, a Goddess. Get your money, but never forget who you really are." Godson told them with a serious tone. The dancer in front of him kissed him on the cheek. "I like you and your conversation. I wanna get to know you." "Maybe," he said. "Yeah maybe," She repeated after him, looking into his eyes. Before she walked away, he told her, "Peace Goddess."

"So how long you gon be in West Virginia?" Wise asked Sophia. They stepped away from his large entourage and all the strippers so they could have some privacy to talk. "Honestly, I really don't know," she answered. Wise was captivated by her beauty. The black dress she wore exposed a lot of cleavage. It also had holes in the side giving him glimpses of her hips and cheeks. "Can I help you decide?" Wise asked playfully. "Right now I'm just escaping an abusive relationship, thanks to the feds locking him up." Wise just listened to her go into detail about her 3-year bizarre relationship. After listening to her, Wise asked her if she was ready for a real man.

"Right now I'm just enjoying my freedom. I don't think I trust men that much anymore, not even a tall, handsome one such as yourself," she said. "Trust is earned, and time is needed to earn it. So I ask you, will you give me the time I need to earn your trust? Can we become friends?" Wise asked. Sophia looked into his eyes as if she was looking for something. "Do you know how to be a friend?" She asked, after being silent for several seconds. "You've never had a friend like me," he said with a smile.

Chapter VII

"Some niggaz just don't give a fuck and he one of em," Dae Dae stated. "So he one of them hard niggaz huh? We gon see how hard he is when we snatch his mama up." Dae Dae just started laughing. As he drove, he began contemplating putting Wayne on his squad. Dae Dae already had a strong team of robbers, something Cincinnati hadn't seen in a long time. "Yo, slide through the hood," Wayne told him. They were riding down Burnet Ave. when Wayne saw Kelvin standing in front of the barbershop. He was rocking a red fur and he was talking to

Squirl from Prospect. "Look at this nigga. Who da fuck he think he is?! Bitch ass nigga. Pull over right quick." Wayne said, ready to kill Kelvin right there in front of everyone. "Chill nigga. We ain't moving like that we gon get them niggaz tho'. You know word is they moved Baby to a nursing home out of state. They say he paralyzed," Dae Dae went on. "Fuck that bitch ass nigga," Wayne spat. "We need to find out where he at so I can finish his ass!" Wayne responded. "I got something better for you," Dae Dae said with a smirk. "How bout we get the Gudda nigga? He got a spot in Walnut Hills, on Concord." "Hell yeah!" Wayne said, getting excited at the thought. "That cock sucka and his mama got to get it! But I'm a fuck her before I kill her." Dae Dae started laughing, "You sick my nigga." As they rode past, Kelvin continued his conversation. "Call me bruh, in 20 minutes, I'm about to go put it together for you," Kelvin gave Squirrel dap then walked to his Yukon Denali SUV. Before pulling off he fired up a blunt. He made the short drive to Slimes spot on Northern Ave. When he got in front of the house he called Slime and told him to come outside. While he waited, he smoked his blunt, constantly looking in the rear and side mirrors. Slime didn't walk straight to his truck, he paused on the porch taking his time to light up a cigarette, simultaneously he surveyed the street. Satisfied all was well, only then did he walk to Kelvin's truck. "You a paranoid nigga," Kelvin said, as Slime was getting inside the SUV. "Naw blood, if you missed something I'm a see it, nah mean?" Slime gave him some dap once he was situated in the passenger seat. "Aye I got a play for half a brick," Kelvin informed him. Slime pulled out his cellphone and chirped his sister's boyfriend. Since Baby's accident Slime had to go back to doing business with his sister's boyfriend. Only now he was bringing him way more money. Kelvin, Fred, and several other guys from the hood were all going through him now. "I'm at the spot," was all Slime needed to hear. That meant come to the spot. Kelvin pulled off and drove to Clifton where Todd's (Slime's sister's boyfriend) spot was. Todd was familiar with Kelvin, so Kelvin entered the house with Slime. Todd was in his early thirties and was always on point. He moved like he knew he was under surveillance. "What up lil bruh?!" Todd asked, getting up from where he was sitting on the couch and dapped Slime and Kelvin up. "We need a half bruh," Slime told him. "It's only one joint left, y'all might as well take the whole thing and I'll see y'all in a few days when shit back in motion," Todd replied. Instead of leaving with a half brick they ended up with a whole one. They left Todd's spot and went back to Slime's spot. "What you gon do to it?" Slime asked, as they sat in his living room. "I'ma get us a free brick and a half. I gotta go see The Professor. I wish I knew the ingredients to that cut he be making." Kelvin responded. "Hell yea, he be killing em! Just selling cut $250 dollars a ounce. It probably ain't cost him no more than 2-3 hundred to make a brick of that shit. I'm telling you he getting something from his job and mixing it with something." Slime went on. "Just think, them mufuckaz at the zoo be shooting them animals up with some shit. Ain't no telling what that nigga getting his hands on!" Kelvin thought about what Slime had said for a few minutes. If he could get his hands on some of the dope they were getting from Vivica's people and mix it with the cut that Professor was selling, he could put a 2 or 3 on each brick and it would still be fire. Kelvin told Slime that he would be right back. Dae Dae was coming down Northern when Kelvin walked to his truck and got in.

When Kelvin saw the black Mercedes Benz Jeep, he remembered seeing it ride by the barbershop earlier when he was talking to Squirl. As he got in his Yukon paranoia hit him. "Squirl trying to set me up?!" He thought. He watched the Mercedes make a left on Wilson. Kelvin just sat there analyzing the situation. He was thinking of a million scenarios then his phone started ringing, and out of all people it was Squirl calling him. He really started freaking out. "This bitch ass nigga trying to get me bagged! You bitches ain't smarter than me." Kelvin pulled off and went straight to the phone store and bought another phone. He jumped on I75 South until he got to the I71 North exit. He ended up circling the city for the next hour, smoking blunt after blunt. He called Slime and got him paranoid. Slime left his spot leaving the brick he had just gotten from Todd behind. Kelvin was convinced Squirl was the police. He was blowing his old phone up, calling, and texting him crazy. Kelvin ended up driving to Indiana where he had a 23-

year-old rich white girl that loved him to death. He told Slime that he would link up with him tomorrow morning. Slime was Downtown in Bop's spot telling him about Squirl. "Niggas gotta start boxin' these niggas! That foul shit jeopardizing all of us. I hate police ass niggaz!" Bop said bitterly, after hearing what Slime told him. "You still ain't hear nothing on lil bruh?" Slime asked. "I was just about to ask you the same shit," Bop confessed. "I heard China told Peaches that his people put him in a nursing home somewhere out of town." Slime told him. "Who told you that?" Bop asked. "Kelvin said he heard it at the barbershop." Slime answered. "That shit still got me fucked up. I been keeping my eyes and ears open and ain't none of my people heard nothing about who it was that start bussing at him. Lil bruh was stuntin' on too many niggaz, then when he got drunk you know how he got." Bop's mood suddenly changed. "Yeah man lil bruh was a mufucka." Slime's eyes got misty as they reminisced on crazy moments they spent with Baby. "What up doe, you trying to slide up to my people spot? He got a spot over the bridge where we be gambling and shit. It be some bad hoes in there too." Bop suggested. "What is it a house joint?"

Slime asked. "Naw it's a big ass house out in the boonies where my old head be throwing dice games. He got the hot tubs out back on the deck. It's some real boss shit. Fuck wit me one time. Let me turn you on to how real niggaz do it. The O.G. got me on some other shit." Bop boasted. "Other shit like what?" Slime asked, as he stuffed a blunt. "He got so much shit going on bruh, but he got me investing in stocks. Shit we don't even think about." "Like Wall Street? Nigga them crackaz be pulling too much sneaky shit. If I'ma jack some money off, I'ma do the jacking." Bop just laughed. "See, thinking like that is why we missing out and why School and his niggaz, niggaz you done seen mass times, sitting on millions. They gettin' money from all angles, so when ain't no dope in they ain't trippin, they somewhere chilling, still getting to the cheese because they got other shit going... bigger shit." Bop tried to convince Slime. "I can't invest my money in something I don't know about. I'm just being a hunnid." Slime said, thinking of all the scams and swindles he had heard about Wall Street on the news. "Scared money don't make no money bruh, and you can learn the market easy, he been teaching me. You heard of Warren Buffet right?" Bop asked. "That's the rich dude, one of the greatest investors ever. He started with just $100.00 and now he worth billions," Bop continued. Slime was becoming interested now. He agreed to accompany Bop. Almost 2 hours later Bop pulled up to a mini mansion in Florence, Kentucky. Slime had never been in this part of Kentucky, let alone at a house this big. He noticed several expensive cars and trucks parked in the long driveway. Bop saw the fascination all over Slimes face. "Told you my nigga. This big boy shit. You about to sit with the bosses, the niggaz getting real money." When they got to the door it opened and a tall, gorgeous, blonde-haired, white woman with big breasts opened the door wearing a 2-piece swimsuit. "Hello gentlemen may I take your coats?" She said. Slime shed his leather Pelle Pelle, Bop followed suit. "This way." The white woman said and turned around giving them full view of her ass. She led them down a marble floored foyer. In the center of the foyer there was a fountain, an identical replica of the movie Scarface. She led them to a room where there were a dozen women, all dressed in 2 pieces and heels, alongside 5 men who were sitting at a large card table. Slime recognized RoRo immediately, but the other 4 men he had never seen before.

All 5 men were older. One of them had grey braids straight to the back, along with a grey beard and grey mustache. "Aye young blood," they greeted him. "What up O. G's," Bop responded, then gave each one of them a firm handshake. "This my lil brother Slime he 100. RoRo you already know him, right?" "Yea, what up Slime?" RoRo said, extending his hand. "What up big bruh?" Slime replied, while shaking RoRo's hand. RoRo began introducing him to the other 4 men inside the large room. "This right here is the Godfather of Memphis, just call him Pops." (Pops was the grey haired one). "And this fat, country nigga here is Charlie, we call him Charlie Hustle. He from Atlanta. And this is the Black Al Capone, Face, from Chicago. Lastly, this Easy. Easy looked familiar to Slime, but he couldn't remember where he knew him from. "Welcome to the clubhouse," RoRo said smiling. Slime glanced around the room. There were large flat screen TVs mounted on 3 walls. The biggest fish tank Slime had ever seen in his life was built inside the 4th wall. It was full of an assortment of colorful, exotic, tropical fish. Slime was so busy checking out the decor and the architecture of the house that he was clueless to the way the women were staring at his tattooed face. "The youngsta got all the ladies staring at him like he a rare animal on display at the zoo," Face said with a chuckle. "What we doing poker? Dice? It don't matter to me," Bop suggested. "Pick your poison," RoRo replied. Slime turned to the men. "Aye what's up with them?" He asked nodding towards the women. "They're here to entertain you, so just tell them what you want." Godfather said. "This yo spot?" Slime asked. "This is our clubhouse." Godfather said, correcting him. "O.G., I was schooling him to the stock market game, telling him some of the things you told me." Bop said knowing Godfather would go into more detail on what he was trying to tell Slime before they got there. "Like I told him. That shit for white people, niggaz ain't investing in shit they don't know about. Ain't no niggaz on Wall Street." Slime said foolishly. "See, that's the mentality that keeps niggaz boxed in. Damn niggaz can't see the big picture because they so busy thinking small. Blacks had their own Wall Street in

Oklahoma. I'm talking banks, farms, everything they needed to sustain their own economy. And it was doing better than the white folks. The stock market is just a hustle for the advanced hustlers with an understanding on how businesses and companies operate. The dope game is for short term riches with a consequence of long-term prison time if you don't know what you're doing. You gotta know that? It's all about investing your money intelligently. Buying cheap and selling high. The catch is knowing when to buy and knowing when to sell. Let me ask you something youngin'. If you got 100 kilos of coke, are you just gon front 'em out to anybody? Or are you gonna do your research and see who moving what? You got nickel and dime hustlaz, ounce hustlaz, and the weight pushers. Who you gon wanna learn more about? That's how the stock market works. You gotta be smart with your money, never rely on just one hustle. The more pots you got your hand in the more money you gon make." Godfather admonished the youngin'. Slime felt like a lame now after the O.G. finished teaching. Godfather had him wanting to read up on The Black Wall Street in Oklahoma. "So, I can go chill with the ladies?" Slime asked with a smile.

"This nigga a pimp." Slime said to himself as he made his way

over to the beautiful selection of women.

Chapter VIII

"Real talk my nigga, you know I ain't bout to say no shit like that just to be saying it." "Good looking my nigga, I appreciate it." Squirl said into the phone. "Aight my nigga. I'm a get up wit you in a minute," he said. "See you in a minute fool," Squirl said before ending the call. He sat there in his living room staring out into space, thinking about what he was just told. This was serious. His name was everything to him and for Kelvin to throw dirt on it was something he couldn't let go. "What's wrong baby?" His girlfriend asked as she entered the living room with their dinner for the night. "I'm cool," Squirl lied. He thought about how Kelvin had stopped answering his phone and now his number was out of service. Being labeled a rat was something he couldn't stomach, especially when he hadn't done what he was accused of. Now they were spreading the rumor through the hood. "Fuck dat nigga," he said as he sat his plate on the coffee table hard. "Baby what's going on?! Talk to me Quinten," she asked becoming worried. "I'll be back later."

Squirl said. "I need to take care of something." He said while he grabbed his jacket and walked out the door.

Slime wanted to believe that Kelvin didn't have anything to do with his spot getting broken into, but nobody else knew he had the brick in there. He spent all night in Florence with Bop coincidently the same night someone decides to hit the spot? Hell nah! He didn't believe in coincidences. When he confronted Kelvin, Kelvin immediately got defensive. Giving him another reason to be suspicious of him. He began thinking the entire "Squirl trying to set him up" was a decoy. "Man fuck dat nigga, what I look like breaking into his spot? I ain't got to. Just think about it Bop? I'm a turn 1 into 2, serve Squirl a half and have a brick and a half left to play wit? It's free money! For Slime to even think some shit like that got me salty on some real shit my nigga!" Kelvin exclaimed. Bop understood where Kelvin was coming from so he told him that he would talk to Slime for him. Kelvin, Bop, and Fred were sitting in the bar and grill in Newport, Kentucky having drinks and discussing the situation. They stayed in the bar until around 11:00pm, then they all went their separate ways. Kelvin called up one of his new, young, playheads from Evanston and told her he was sliding through. He needed to get some more weed first though, he was down to one blunt which he rolled up as he headed to the hood. When he got to Dread's spot on Prospect Ave., Dread pulled out a new batch of Kush that he had on him. Kelvin copped a whole zip and headed on his mission. He was at the light on Harvey and Rockdale talking to his young girl on the phone when he looked over and saw the window rolled down on a red mustang. Once he saw the face of the driver he tried to grab his gun, but, it was too late.........

"Bop wake yo fat ass up!" Sharee said, shaking Bop out of his sleep. It was the tone of her voice that alerted him that something was wrong. "What's up, what's wrong?!" He asked, rolling over and opening his eyes. "Look," she pointed at the flat screen tv. Bop sat up in his spacious California king bed and focused in on the television. For a second he wondered what was so important, then he saw Kelvin's mugshot appear on the television. He couldn't hear what they were saying but he saw the Yukon that Kelvin had just bought with the driver's side door opened and crashed on the sidewalk. He knew what that had meant. The first person that came to his mind was Slime. "Dam!" He said, as he grabbed his cellphone off the nightstand to call him. Slime answered on the second ring. "What up?" Bop asked. Slime already knew why Bop was calling. His girl was getting ready for work when she saw the story about a man being gunned down in his SUV in Avondale late last night.

"Yo, that shit wild, I just seen it. My girl woke me up and been crying ever since," Slime said. Bop didn't know if Slime was spinning him or not. He knew he would have to see him face to face to tell. "Aight bra, I'm a get up with you when I come out." Slime said. "Aight I'm bout to try to call bruh baby mama. I know she sick, damn!" Bop said. By the time the sun had come up, word was spreading through the streets that Slime had gotten Kelvin killed over a brick of heroin. Fred was going crazy. Kelvin was like his younger brother. He wasn't trying to talk about anything to anyone. All he was on was finding Slime; and putting a bullet in his head. "You need to just stay in the house, cause ain't nothing but trouble outside! You know you didn't do that shit. You ain't gotta prove yourself to nobody!" Slime thought about what his pregnant girlfriend was saying. She was right, but he knew how it would look in the hood if he stayed away. "I got to baby. If I don't its gon look suspicious." Slime tried to convince her. Ladona began crying. "I'm begging you Jacob, please just stay here with me." She pleaded, calling him by his birth name. Slime hugged her and then knelt to kiss his unborn child in her stomach. "I gotta go," he said. Ladona's tears turned into sobs. She knew how the game was played. She had lost both of her brothers to the streets. After Slime walked out the door all she could think about was her child growing up without a father. It crushed her. Slime pulled up in front of Kelvin's mother's house on Glenwood Ave. Not knowing what to expect, he had his bullet proof vest on. Two .40 caliber pistols with 30 round magazines adorned each side of his waist. He got out of his car and walked to the front door and rang the doorbell. When the door opened, instead of Kelvin's mother it was Kelvin's older sister standing there. He knew she had heard the rumors that were circling throughout the hood by the way she was looking at him. He spoke. "I felt I had to come here in person and look y'all in the eyes and tell y'all I had nothing to do with Kelvin's death. The rumors ain't true. Kelvin was like a brother to me. My spot did get broken into and yea me and bruh got into a argument but I swear to you on my kids I didn't do that shit." Tanae stared into his eyes and something in her gut told her that he was telling the truth. She threw her arms around him and started bawling like a baby. Her tears brought her mother to the door. Slime looked her in her eyes and told her the same thing, that he didn't kill her son or have anything to do with it. He sat with Tanae and her mother for nearly an hour, then he drove around the corner to the barbershop. Although it was freezing cold outside, people were huddled up in front of the shop. Ace was talking to his client when he saw Slime get out of his car. He had heard the same rumor everyone else had heard and it saddened him. First, Baby and Low and now Kelvin. He had watched them all grow up on the block. When they were barely keeping a dollar in their pocket everything was okay, but as soon as the money started coming in they started killing each other. Slime didn't speak to any of the people giving him cold stares as he entered the shop. "Yo Ace, what up can I get a cut?" Ace along with everyone else in the shop looked at him with a funny look on their faces. "Look, I'm a say this shit one time since all you mufuckaz looking at me like I'm the devil. I didn't do that shit and I ain't have nothing to do with it! And I'm telling y'all right now if it's between me and any one of you mufuckaz I'm choosing me!" Slime stood there with his hands in his red, leather, Pelle Pelle coat, gripping his bangers ready to back up what he had said. Ace excused himself from his clients and pulled Slime to the rear of the shop. "Right now I think you should go chill and let the truth come out. It ain't about not being a hoe or a bitch, it's about being smart. This shit crazy. It's like yall dropping back-to-back. The shit y'all out here thinking is a game ain't a game at all. For every action, there's a reaction. So you gotta think before you move, and right now you moving reckless. You know what you are and what you did or didn't do." Slime stood there listening to Ace bless him with wisdom.

"Look at Baby? Laying up in a nursing home, somewhere in a coma. Low dead. Them boys was like brothers. This game is evil. It turns fathers against sons, mothers against daughters, brothers against brothers. I sell my weed and I go in the house. I know what's waiting for me out there. Nothing but jealousy, envy, and a bunch of miserable mufuckaz trying to tear me down because I'm doing what they don't have the discipline and patience to do. You gotta understand your surroundings.

Them niggaz who been out there they whole lives and still ain't got shit don't like seeing y'all come through iced up and driving the cars they dream of driving. Wearing the clothes they wish they had. Right now they rooting for you to get killed. Then they gon show up at your funeral talking bout 'damn I miss my nigga Slime he was a real nigga'." "You absolutely right my nigga. I'ma catch up with you in a couple weeks. I think I'm gon take a vacation with my girl. Thanks for dropping them jewels on me." Slime told him. We all need to hear words of encouragement from time to time." Ace said. Slime called Ladona and told her he was on his way home. As he walked to the door of the shop the sidewalk had cleared. A few of the

people that were standing outside were now inside soaking up

the heat. Slime walked outside the shop and paused to light up a

cigarette. He caught sudden movement from his peripheral.

From where he was inside the shop Ace saw the entire thing

unfold. Slime spun to his right as a masked man started firing on

him, no further than 15 feet away. He yanked both .40's out of

his pockets and started blazing back. Bullets slammed into his

torso, almost knocking him off his feet. Slime didn't know if the

bullets pierced the bullet proof vest or not. Just when he saw the

shooter in front of him go down, gun shots came from behind

him slamming into his back. He felt the impact of each bullet.

He spun around firing. It was like he was playing a video game.

He zeroed in on his target and kept firing until he saw him go

down, then he surveyed the street looking for any other

potential threats to eliminate. It wasn't until he relaxed that he

dropped to one knee barely able to breathe. "Fuck man! I'm

about to die," He thought. Ace ran to him from the shop. "You

need to lay down. I don't know how you still alive." Ace had

watched bullet after bullet slam into his upper body. "Help me take my jacket off." Slime said, in between breaths. Ace helped

him remove his jacket, then the hooded sweatshirt he wore

underneath it. When he saw the vest, he smiled. "You good my

nigga, you gotta get up out of here before the police come. That

was self-defense remember that." Ace told him. Slime stumbled

to his car and drove off, leaving two dead bodies twisted up on

the cold sidewalk.

Chapter IX

"I really appreciate how nice you've been treating me for the last couple of months, but I need to be honest with you because I really do like you." Sophia told Wise, as she gazed into his brown eyes. "You can always be honest with me." Wise told her as he grabbed her, savoring the intimate moment. "Damn girl you so beautiful," Wise said, admiring her gorgeous face. She blushed and lowered her gaze. "Wise... I'm pregnant by my ex. I know I told you he was in jail fighting a federal case but what I didn't tell you is, I ran off with a lot of his dope and jewelry. I don't have anyone I can trust. Can I trust you Wise?" She spoke. "Yes, you can trust me." Wise said, but in his mind he was wondering how much dope she had. "I wanna get some money together and give half to my ex's mother for his other children. Then I want to get me a house and put some money up so me and my baby will be okay." They sat in Red Lobster and finished having lunch. Wise had not expected their date to go this good. The heroin and cocaine that Rasta was supplying him with was good for sure, but one could never have enough product. Wise began formulating a scheme to get the dope from her for free, or at least next to free. "How much dope is it?" He asked her. "It's a lot," she answered him. "Where is it?" He went on. Sophia smiled at him. "Come on now, I'm not that stupid," she said. Wise started laughing. "First help me sell the jewelry, then I'll give you some of the dope to test out or whatever you do with it, and we can go from there, deal?" "Deal," he said. "Shake on it," Sophia said, extending her hand. Wise shook her hand with a firm grip. They finished eating their lunch and Wise took her back to her hotel, where they remained for the rest of the day.

"Peace God." Godson said, greeting Wise as he walked into the City Park apartment the next afternoon. "Peace." Wise said, returning the greeting. "What up with you God? Ever since you hooked up with that Sophia chick you don't even fuck wit the Gods no more," Science said jokingly. "Yo son, I'm feeling shortie I can't lie. She something different." Wise admitted. "She a good look for you," Science said. "Yo. I ran into one of them niggaz from Saint Albans at the gas station. It took everything in me not to burn that nigga. Im getting tired of this sitting around shit, just cause we getting money. Money can't bring Ramon back! Yall act like y'all forgot these niggaz killed one of us." Godson barked on them. "Son listen to me," Wise said. "We just tied into a major plug now. Everybody got to deal with us. We controlling the market from here on out. This just the first shipment. We can't fuck that up. We gone handle them niggaz. Let time pass let them niggaz get comfortable and that's when we hit em. Until then, we gotta get dis money yo!" Godson just shook his head, as if he disagreed. By the days, he was beginning to feel as if Ramon's death wasn't that important to Wise. Godson didn't want to believe that Wise played a part in Ramon's death, but it was beginning to look that way.

***

Black lay in Keoka's bed panting after Keoka gave him her body for breakfast. "Damn girl! It should be a first-degree felony to have pussy that dam good." Keoka giggled. "Boy shut up!"

She laughed and then leaned over and kissed him on the lips. Black admired her heart shaped ass when she got out of the bed and put on her satin robe. "I'll be right back." Keoka told him. Keoka went to the bathroom to make the call she had been ordered to make. She was terrified, but she had no choice. She had been approached last week, by what she thought was a baller from Chicago, at the club she danced at. The next day he picked her up for a date and that's when she learned his true reason for approaching her.

To keep him from killing her she told him about Black being responsible for Ramon's death, and how he had threatened to get her little brother killed if she didn't help him. So here she was again caught up in the middle of something she didn't want to be involved in. She started some bath water in the tub then she walked back to her bedroom where Black was talking on his cellphone. "Come on, I'm running us some bath water," she commanded him. "Aye you just make sure them little niggaz have that paper today… Every penny, or it's yo ass in the cooker you hear me nigga?! I'm not playing Freddy." Black said

Freddy's name on purpose so Keoka could hear how he was giving out orders. Freddy was a well-known hustler from Orchard Manor. Black was now supplying him via Wise. Wise had put him in charge of the Orchard Manor operations. It was his job to make sure the money was always correct. After ending the call, Black grabbed a Newport and lit it up. "Come 'mere girl." He said. "Grab that money outta my jeans for me." Keoka did as she was told. She handed Black the extra large wad of cash. "You know it ain't nothing you can't have now. You mine now girl. If I ball, you ball, ya hear me..." He began making it rain on her. Keoka dropped to her knees and with no hands she took him into her mouth. "Mmm," she moaned. She was taking her time purposely. Black had no idea what was coming his way.

Baby, LJ, Flip, and Scooter were all silent as LJ drove the Buick SUV. It had been two long months, but it was well worth the wait. At first Wise was their target up until a week ago. Baby had done some investigating and baited Keoka into a trap. She identified the person behind his cousin's death as Black. He wanted to get the deed over with so that they could get back to

Cincinnati. LJ got a call from his mother informing him of Kelvin's death. Then days later Slime caught two bodies and the police were now looking for him. Kelvin's death hit Baby hard. He tried to push it to the back of his mind and focus on the task at hand.

Keoka lived in a cul-de-sac right next to the projects. "Why you bring your gun in the bathroom boy?" Keoka asked, as if he didn't need it. "Gotta keep my hammer in arms reach. You never know when shit gon jump off," Black said proudly. "So you running things now I see? What about the rest of the New York niggaz? What if they find out you the one who killed Ramon? You ain't worried about them retaliating?" Keoka asked, while washing his back. "Don't worry about them," Black told her. "What you mean? I ain't trying to have niggaz shooting up my house. I got children to protect Black." Black responded cockily. "They ain't gon do shit to me! How you think I found out you was transporting for them niggaz?" If Black could have seen all the color drain out of her face, he would have known Keoka was up to something. For her sake, his back was towards her face. Ramon was setup by his own

crew, Keoka thought. She continued washing him up. When he

turned around, she turned her back to him so that he wouldn't

be able to look into her eyes. "Your turn, wash my back," she

said, handing him the wash rag.

"Me and LJ going in through the backdoor. She left it unlocked

for us." Baby said. "Flip, you and Scooter hold us down in the

front." "You know I got you big bruh." Flip assured him. 'Come

on bruh," Baby commanded, as he exited the car followed by

LJ. They walked briskly to the back of the house. "Where you

going?" Keli asked her brother Wan. "I gotta go grab something

out of Keoka's house." He responded. "She ain't there, that's

why I'm up here." Keli said, knowing what was going on at her

sister's house. Keoka had come to her after Baby gave her the

choice to either help him kill Black or die for him. "I ain't gotta

go inside, I hid something in her backyard," Wan said. "You

can't go down there at all Wan!" Something in his sister's voice

got his attention.

"What's going on Keli? I ain't worried about them niggaz doing nothing to me, fuck them niggaz," Wan said, and pulled out his .45 semi-automatic. He showed his sister that he was strapped. Despite her warning he walked out of their mother's apartment. He walked to the trail that led down the side of the hill to his sister's street.

Keoka walked naked to her bedroom with Black behind her. "Damn boy, put that gun down and put this lotion on my back," she demanded. Black sat his gun on her dresser and grabbed the bottle of lotion she handed him. To get him as far as she could from his gun she walked to her bed and laid on her stomach. Black stood over her enjoying the beautiful sight of her nude backside. Hungrily, he began applying lotion to her body. "Ooh your hands feel good." Keoka moaned loudly. LJ put his finger to his lips and pointed up the stairs. Baby shook his head as an affirmative. LJ crept up the stairs while Baby followed closely behind. They were in a city they had never even been in before now, about to commit murder. LJ prayed everything went as they planned, as butterflies entered his stomach. "This nigga killed my cousin and dumped his body in the woods," was the only thing on Baby's mind. Once they reached the top of the stairs, they heard moaning coming from the room Keoka told him was her bedroom. The floor creaked loudly as LJ neared the door and they stopped abruptly. Black had Keoka on her hands and knees eating her pussy from the back while she bounced her ass in his face. When LJ made the floor creak Black stopped what he was doing. "Fuck was that?" He asked. "Don't stop Daddy, I'm about to cum." Keoka whined. "Hold up." Black said, then got up to retrieve his gun. Baby heard what Black said and decided to rush in. The bedroom door flew open and Keoka shrieked! Black had a look of death on his face. He lunged for his gun. Baby started bussing him with the .357 Python that he clutched. Keoka dove to the floor and began crawling to the doorway. Once she got to the hallway she ran and never looked back. "You thought you got away with it huh?! Bitch ass nigga!" Baby said with venom. Black was on the floor still trying to reach his gun. Baby kicked him in his ass. "Fuck all this movie shit," LJ said, and shot him in the back of the head two times. "Let's go bruh!" Wan was coming out of the trail when he saw his sister running down the street naked and screaming. Seconds later he saw the Buick Rendezvous pulling up. Wan locked eyes with Scooter just as Flip was rolling the window down to kill Keoka. "Naw that's my niggas with her. If she get on some police shit I'll take care of her myself." Scooter said. Wan saw the Mac-90 coming out of the window and pulled his gun. Keoka stepped in front of her younger brother. "Please don't kill him!" She begged. Flip waited for Baby to give him the order. "Let's go." Baby told LJ, and LJ sped off.

Chapter X

Wise was furious that Black got killed. Not because he really cared, but because it threatened to unfold his entire operation. He sent word for Mannie to come to his spot. While he waited, he weighed his options. Black had the influence he needed to keep all his workers in line. He had enough power to keep them from getting any "bright ideas". The only other person who had that type of influence was the young boy Scooter, but Scooter wasn't fucking with him. Scooter was the only one he felt could fill Black's shoes. When Mannie finally got there he had three of his cousins with him. "What's going on Mannie? How could something like that happen?! I wanna know how, and who?" Wise snapped. "We tryna figure that out," Mannie said.

"Only niggaz we had beef wit is them niggaz from Huntington and the niggaz from St. Albans." "We got to send a message, let these niggaz know we ain't playing! Go tear St. Albans up! They trying to fuck up the money and I can't have that. Ain't nobody

fuckin' up my money, you hear me my nigga, NOBODY!"
Unlike Black, Mannie was intimidated by Wise and his New
York crew. Black was the backbone of his crew and without his
presence, none of his crew members had the guts or balls to do
the things he made them do on their own. "Get some of them lil
niggas that wanna be down and make them put in some work.
Make them prove they self." Wise added. Godson sat quietly but
inside he was fuming. He observed Wise. Here he was ready to
shed blood over losing Black, but no one had been held
accountable for Ramon's death. He began to see clearly what
was up. Wise and Black's alliance wasn't by coincidence. "And
get word to Scooter that I want to see him!" Wise barked. After
Mannie and his crew left, Wise paced the tiny apartment trying
to predict the future. The ringing of his cellphone caused him to
stop pacing. He looked at the number and saw that it was his
baby mama back home in New York. Wise didn't have the
patience or self-control to deal with her in that moment, so he
sent her to voicemail. Five minutes later his cell phone rang
again. This time it was Sophia. "Yo?" He answered, in an
agitated tone. "Dang, what I do baby?" Sophia asked, noticing

his demeanor. "It ain't you, I'm just dealing with something right now." He explained. "What's up?" "I got one of the watches. I wanted you to see it first before Grace shows this guy she knows," she said. "Where you at?" Wise asked. "I'm at the Embassy still," she answered. "Oh ok, I'll be down there in a second, wait for me." He told her. "Hurry up baby," she said as she hung up. "Aye, I gotta check out this shit Sophia got right quick. Godson ride wit me," Wise commanded. "And Science, if Scooter come through keep him here." As they walked out of the apartment, Wise saluted his security that he had posted in the hallways. "Y'all keep holding it down aight? I'll be back in a second." "We out here my nigga. And if a nigga come through here acting wrong we gon straighten his ass up." The chubby faced kid said. When they got outside in the cold January weather, everyone they passed by greeted them as if they were their idols. "You see that shit nigga? These mufuckaz love us. We feeding these niggas, so they'll do anything we tell them to do." Wise boosted. Wise didn't ride around in expensive cars, he kept it simple. They got into an F150, extended cab pickup truck. "Yo Wise, level wit me God," Godson spoke. Wise looked over at Godson with curious eyes.

"What up son? What's on your mind?" "This whole thing with Ramon yo… I been doing the math and shit ain't adding up. Son didn't move reckless at all. Only way he could've gotten hit was with inside help." Godson said, as he turned to face Wise. Wise slid his hand down to his waist. "Yo son, you buggin' baby." Wise said with a smile. "What's done is done. I just need to know so I can relax. Don't leave me in the dark son. Yo, I been lookin at these corny ass niggaz ready to flat they heads thinking one of them killed our mans," Godson went on. "Yo son, sometimes in order for us to rise in this game… We gotta make sacrifices God," Wise said while he looked him straight in the eyes.

He was ready to blaze his man that he had grew up with since a shorty if he had made any sudden move or said the wrong thing. "Peace God." Godson said, in so many words telling Wise he didn't want any beef. Wise started the truck up and pulled off.

***

"Just hang in there a little while longer. Didn't you tell me you was gon help me get back on my feet?" Baby spoke into the phone. "Yea but this nigga really beginning to think he my man. He getting all clingy and shit." Jazzy said pouting, with her face in a frown. "I wanna hit this nigga for everything, so I need you to keep making him feel comfortable baby." He told her. "He been feeling like that since I sold him your watch," she explained. "Look, I gotta slide back to Cincinnati and see what's going on with Slime. Plus, I wanna go to Kelvin's funeral," he said. "Hell naw! You ain't leaving me down here by myself Baby," Jazzy protested. "You're not by yourself, Flip gon be down here with you." Baby said, trying to make her feel better. "I feel like you pimping me out." She began crying. "Do you hear how crazy you sound? I just lost over a million dollars! I still owe your brother and my connect. You said you was down. This is for us, for our son. Stop crying and get yourself together. This can't be the Jazzy I fell in love with. I heard females be on some emotional shit when they pregnant so I'ma let you slide." He said, using reverse psychology on her. "I don't know what's wrong with me, it's my hormones." She sobbed. "I love you girl, never doubt that do you hear me?" Baby said. "Yeah I hear you," she answered. "Okay then. Now help me get this paper." Baby said, ending the call.

After ending the phone call with Jazzy, Baby walked downstairs where LJ, Scooter, Flip, and Ashley were. The two months that they had spent in Ashley's home brought her and her children close to him. Baby considered them family now. "Scooter, you and Flip walk with me out back for a minute." Baby said and started walking towards the back door. Scooter and Flip followed Baby out to Ashley's backyard. Baby rolled up a blunt before he began speaking. "Yo Scooter, I appreciate your loyalty and I promise you this shit is only the beginning. I need you to get all the way in with Wise and his crew. That way when I knock him off you can fill his spot. Don't worry about nothing else. Learn his operation so when it comes time for you to run it you can. Flip, I want you to just be a ghost. If any situation arises, I want you to take care of it. That nigga Wise too smart for his own good. If Jazzy calls you and she's in trouble you get to her. Im entrusting you with my bitch and my son lil bruh."

Baby said, looking him in his eyes. "Come on Baby you know I got you." Flip said. "We gone take this whole shit over, all I need is yall to trust me!"

"I know how you rock big bruh and I'm right here beside you." Flip started. "All I seen so far was real nigga shit from you, so I'm with you too." Scooter added. "Aight yall hold it down. I'm a see yall when I get back." Baby went back into the house to say his goodbye to Ashley.

"Yo Marlyn, you said these niggas was on some legit shit," he said. "Chill Dae Dae. You know you my nigga, they cool," he responded. Dae Dae was impatient. He hated waiting. When Marlyn saw the silver Lincoln Navigator bending the corner he smiled. "What I tell you? There they go right there." Marlyn said, pointing to the Navigator. Marylyn got out of Dae Dae's black Mercedes Benz Jeep with the two bricks of heroine that Dae Dae had tapped danced all over in tow. Dae Dae watched Marlyn tell the driver of the Navigator to step out of the truck. It was crazy how Marlyn, one of his lowkey robbing partners, was blood cousins with Baby. Dae Dae knew firsthand that Marlyn was cutthroat. He smiled as he thought about the time that he and Marlyn ran in on Baby while he was in the bed sleeping. Then later down the line Marlyn found out Baby was his first cousin. Every nigga that Dae Dae hung with was a snake, which was why he formed a secret conglomerate of jack boys dubbed "Sic" Snakes in Cahoots. Robbery, kidnapping, murder-for-hire, they did it all. Dae Dae observed Marlyn and the driver of the Navigator getting into the truck. 10 minutes later Marlyn was walking back to his jeep with a footlocker bag containing $275k.

"What I tell you, hoe ass nigga?!" Marlyn said, with a grin on his face. "Yo, take me out my sister's house." Marlyn said. Marlyn called his sister and told her he was on his way out there. "Baby! Marlyn just called me and said he was on his way over here." China said. "That's cool," Baby responded, "me and bruh bout to roll out anyway." "Don't forget to call Frankie. She said whatever she had to talk to you about was important." China reminded Baby. "I got you. My word," he promised. Before leaving, LJ and Baby went to China's son

Lamar's room and roughed him up until he started crying.
"Shut yo punk ass up lame." LJ teased him. "Fuck you bitch!"
Lamar spat, which gained him another punch to his chest.
China ran upstairs after hearing her son screaming at the top of
his lungs. "What y'all do to my got damn son?!" She screamed.
"That bad ass nigga need to get roughed up, he soft." Baby told
her.

"You soft, bitch ass nigga!" Lamar spat. "Boy what I tell you
about talking like that?" China reprimanded. "Watch your
mouth!" LJ and Baby laughed at him as his mother disciplined
him for his foul language. "Now come on lame. I'm a buy you
some shoes." Baby told him after China was finished with him.
Hearing Baby say those magic words, he stopped crying on a
dime. When they got out to LJ's car LJ told Baby that Slime's
baby mama had texted back. "Call her." Baby said. LJ made
the call as he backed out of China's driveway. "Ladona, this me.
Hold up..." LJ said and handed Baby the phone to speak. "Sis
what's good?" "Who is this?!" Ladona asked with frustration.
"Damn, you done forgot all about lil bruh already?" Baby said.

"Baby?? Oh my god!" Ladona said, shocked. "Chill sis. I don't want mufuckas to know I'm out my coma. I'm trying to get in contact with Bruh though." Baby told her. "I'm a have him call you. Let me call him right quick," she said. "Aight. Tell that nigga I don't want mufuckas knowing I'm out my coma." Baby demanded. "Okay, I will." She said and hung up. It took Slime all of 30 seconds to call LJ's phone. "What up bitch!" Baby said, smiling as he answered the phone. "Man! Where the fuck you at?!" Slime asked, clearly excited. "I'm in the city nigga. Where you at?" Baby said.

"I'm in Tennessee over my weird ass cousin's house, smoking this bullshit ass weed man. Y'all gotta come down here and bring me a pound of some real weed." Slime said. "Nigga chill. I got you and I'm a take you somewhere where you'll be aight. Give me a few days, like 3 or 4." Baby told him. "I already had Ladona take a lawyer 35 bands and I paid a private investigator. The lawyer want me to turn myself in but fuck all that shit." Slime said. "I feel you on that," Baby agreed, "Make them mufuckaz do they job. But on another note bruh, what the fuck happened?!" Baby asked, switching topics. "When you get here I'll break it down to you." Slime assured him. "Aight, be easy. Baby to the rescue. You know I'm like Steven Segal, Hard To Kill nigga!" Baby joked, but he was serious. Slime started laughing and ended the call. "Bye fool."

LJ was pulling into the gas station right around the corner from China's house when they saw Dae Dae walking out of the gas station to a black Benz Jeep. LJ pulled to the far end of the parking lot where they could be inconspicuous. Seconds later they watched Marlyn walk out of the gas station and get into the passenger side of the same jeep that Dae Dae had just gotten into. "When your people start hanging with Dae Dae?" LJ asked. "Yo guess good as mine." Baby answered. After Dae Dae pulled out the lot, LJ got out and went inside to buy cigars. Bop was sitting in his normal spot on the block, as always, although these days he never did any dealing hand to hand himself. He still dressed dingy and looked like he was barely getting by, but the streets knew better. A black Range Rover pulled up on the block and stopped in front of the building Bop was in. Bop got a chirp on his phone. "Big Bruh, some nigga named Red from Bond Hill out here. He say he need to holla at you." One of his workers chirped. "Send him in," Bop chirped back. A minute later, a knock came from the apartment door. Rome, Bops doorman, got up and answered it. When Bop saw Red, he smiled. "What up pretty ass nigga?! You coming down to the slums looking like you signed to Icy Entertainment." Bop said. "What up my nigga. I stopped by to put a bug in yo ear." Red said. "What's going on?" Bop asked, the smile now gone from his face. Red looked at Rome. "Unc, go in the back for a minute." Bop told him. "Yo, I know who smoked yo boy Kelvin." Red said.

"Talk to me my nigga." Bop said, picking up a half smoked Black & Mild out of the ash tray and blazing it up. "That nigga Squirl." Red said, staring Bop in his eyes. "How you know for sure my nigga?" Bop asked. "You know he fuck with my cousin. He just tried to get me to serve him a quarter brick of pup. I told him I heard he was working and he told me niggas get killed for putting bad papers on niggas. It was the way he said it and the look in his eyes. I could tell he was salty. What if Kelvin was

wrong about him being the police? I ain't gon lie, a nigga put

papers on me like that I gotta kill you. Ain't nothing to talk

about." Red said, honestly. Bop sat there thinking about what

Red said. There was no denying if a nigga accused a man of

being the police and he really wasn't, he had to die. So that

meant that Slime had been telling the truth. Bop thought. "Bruh

probably was on some high shit and saw something that

spooked him," Bop thought.

It was like Red was reading his thoughts, because he said, "Damn man! That's some ill shit. And you can't blame a nigga for defending his honor and his name." "Shittin' me." Bop fired back, giving him a hard stare. "He still gotta die, fuck that!" "I know you feel like that. I ain't trying to defend the nigga but put yourself in his shoes bruh. What would you do? Kelvin was a good nigga but he brung it on his self." Red said. "I asked that nigga if he was sure when he told me that shit. I called him that night. You know that nigga was a junkie when it came to weed." Bop was sick. His eyes filled with tears as the realization came to him that Kelvin brought his death on his self.

***

Fred couldn't believe it still. He thought Baby was in a nursing home somewhere out of town. "Shit been crazy lil bruh. I know Kelvin wouldn't have backdoored Slime. Lil bruh wasn't cut like that and you know it. Slime people got it right now, so we been going through him. I been coppin' a quarter brick at a time just to keep the phones going." Baby looked Fred in his eyes and could see Kelvin's death weighed heavy on his conscious. "Have you talked to Slime?" Baby asked him. "Ain't nothing to talk about. That bitch boxed 2 of my shooters. When I see him it's on sight! This world ain't big enough for the both of us to co-exist." Fred said, clearly heated. "What if you trippin and Slime ain't the one who killed Kelvin? You jumping to conclusions like somebody did with me, and now Low dead!" Baby snapped. "Do you know who killed Low Fred?" Fred looked from LJ to Baby. "I was with LJ when we seen that shit on the news." Fred answered. "Fuck you trying to say nigga? I had something to do with Low getting wacked?" Baby questioned. "Slime didn't kill Kelvin bruh." Baby continued. "Then who did, and why?" Fred countered. "That's what we gon find out." Baby answered him.

Chapter XI

Gudda had something nice going on with Keith. Keith was

flooding him with bricks of coke and boy and Gudda had

Walnut Hills jumping. With his mother in his ear as his adviser,

he stayed out of the spotlight and under the radar. He only dealt

with a handful of people that he knew he could trust, and Bop

was one of them. "That's some ill shit my nigga." Gudda said,

after listening to Bop tell him about why Kelvin was killed. "Shit

real out here. Even real niggas gotta accept the consequences

for what they do or say. The game ain't bias bruh." Bop said as

he continued counting out the money that he owed Gudda.

"Shit gon be back on next week my people said, so slow roll

whatever you got left." Gudda advised. Bop got up and walked

Gudda to his car. Bop noticed the black Mercedes Jeep sitting in

the same spot it had been sitting in when Gudda pulled up. It

was as if whoever was behind the tinted windows read his mind

because they pulled off seconds after they walked out. "Aye yo

be careful bruh. Did you see that black Mercedes Jeep parked up the street?" Bop asked. "It was right there when I pulled up." Gudda answered. "Shit like that be how niggas get killed." Bop said, not knowing how true his words were. Gudda gave him some dap then got in his car and got up out of there.

"So you think Bop the one supplying that nigga?" Wayne asked. "I don't know, but I do know the Kresha bitch Bop fuck with be with my cousin so it ain't shit for us to catch him over there and snatch his ass. He gotta be worth a couple hunnid." Dae Dae responded. "What up wit you and Marlyn? You keep fuckin' wit dat nigga knowing he related to Baby. Fuck that nigga bruh." Wayne said aggressively. "Nah fam cool, believe me, he 100% wit me. I can't say fuck him, he been wit me since forever bruh. He just found out Baby was his cousin. This between me and you. Marlyn was with me when I ran up in Baby's mama apartment. We hit him for 80 bands and then we hit some bitch that LJ was fucking with and got 30 more." Dae Dae admitted to him. "Still doe... fuck that nigga!" Wayne said. Dae Dae didn't say anything but in his mind he was thinking they just might have to put Wayne in the trick bag.

He began wondering how much would Wayne's life be worth if Fred learned that Wayne was the one that took the contract that Squirl put out on Kelvin's head? Kelvin's death was by choice. They were on Prospect Ave. gambling that night when Squirl came through fuming. He was going on and on about how Kelvin was putting dirt on his name. Being that Squirl was from the hood too and was getting some money, Wayne approached him about what Squirl wanted done. Squirl said he had $20k on Kelvin's head. Later on that same night, Wayne caught Kelvin pulling up to Dread's weed spot to buy some weed and laid on him. When Kelvin pulled off Wayne followed him. He caught him at a red light talking on his cellphone. Dae Dae knew this because Wayne called him right after he committed the murder. "Drop me off to my whip." Wayne said. Dae Dae didn't say anything back, he just headed towards the hood where Wayne's car was parked. As soon as Wayne got in his car he called one of his young goons. "Where you at lil bruh?" Wayne asked. "I'm on Blair. What's up big bruh?" The youngin responded. "Im about to swing through and holla at you." Wayne answered. "Aight I'm on the short end, over my girl people house," he said. "Aight," Wayne said, and hung up. As soon as Dae Dae dropped Wayne off he called Marlyn. "Where you at fool?" "Over my mother house." Marlyn answered. "I'm about to slide up on you. I need to holla at you bout some real shit." Dae Dae said. "See you in a second fool." Maryln replied. Dae Dae drove over to Reading Rd and turned onto long Blair, where Maryln's mother stayed. He had called Maryln as he was turning onto the street so when he pulled up to Ms. Stephanie's house Maryln was already waiting on the porch. "What up fool?" Maryln said, getting into Dae Dae's jeep. "Yo boy Wayne, we might have to get that nigga up through." Dae Dae said calmly. "That ain't my boy, that's yo boy! You know I keep my circle small. I don't even rock with my brother because he fuck wit too many niggaz. What he do tho?" Maryln asked curiously. "That nigga said fuck you because you some kin to Baby. I'm like naw that's my nigga, he official. But he still like fuck that nigga. You know he one of them wild boys ain't no telling what he a do." Dae Dae tried to convince him. Maryln sat quietly analyzing the situation. He wasn't one to sit back and wait for the beef to come to him. "It's on." Maryln said, giving him some dap. "I'm a call you and let you know what's up." Dae Dae told him.

"Aight fool." Maryln said as he got out the jeep. Dae Dae knew what Maryln was thinking.

A lot of people underestimated Maryln because he wasn't loud and wild. He had never seen Maryln's feathers ruffled, he was always cool and calm, even under extreme circumstances. Dae Dae pulled off and headed to Peaches house.

"The nigga basically choosing sides so fuck that nigga too, feel me?" Wayne said. "Hell yea. I feel you big bruh. You know I don't give a fuck about none of these niggaz. If they ain't wit us, they against us," he responded. "I'm a put together a party for Dae Dae two faced ass. But dig, we was laying on that nigga Bop Downtown and Gudda bitch ass pulled up. So either Bop supplying Gudda or Gudda supplying Bop." Wayne announced. "Aye bruh, I just found out my little brother fuckin' Gudda little sister. We can snatch her and hold her for ransom. Nigga gon pay for his little sister before a nigga pay for Bop." The man said. "When you find out your brother was fuckin his sister?" Wayne asked. "Today," he responded. "They supposed to be going to the show tonight wit me and my girl. You know lil bruh square ass ain't on shit so we gon just snatch both of 'em."

"Hell yea." Wayne said smiling. "But let me get back in here, we playing spades. I'm a call you in a couple hours." He said.

"Eli, call me little bruh don't get caught up." Wayne said.

"Come on, fuck I'm a get caught up doing?! Nigga I'm trying to at least get a quarter for that little bitch, and I'm going to cop for the summer! You know what's up nigga." Eli told him, dead serious.

Baby had talked Kelvin's mother into allowing him to view the body earlier in the day on the day of his funeral, so that he wouldn't have to reveal himself to everyone. Baby thought back to when Kelvin and Fred first started rocking with him. Tears rolled down his face. "Damn big bruh… You still supposed to be here, we still got a lot of balling to do." Baby said aloud to him. Baby vowed to avenge his fallen comrade's death. After he viewed the body and said his final goodbyes he stopped to talk to Tania and her mother. He promised them that he would look after them as long as he was breathing. Kelvin's mother could see the sincerity in his eyes.

Baby slipped out of the funeral home and into the rental that LJ was waiting for him in. Hours later while LJ attended the funeral, Baby sit in his hotel room thinking about his mother.

He got a call from his Aunt Lucia and she told him that his Uncle Peire wanted to see him. Baby told her to schedule the visit, or whatever she had to do, and let him know. He ended up dozing off after smoking a blunt to the head.

***

"Who is he Carrol?" Detective Washington demanded. "Why Greg?! You think I don't know you've been screwing your partner huh? I hired a private investigator, I have evidence. So how do you want to do this? We can split on nice terms, or it can get ugly?" Carrol threatened. Greg thought about Carrol's money. She had inherited a chunk of it when her mother finally passed. Carrol knew that he was thinking about her money. "You can have the money we invested in the stock market," she told him, knowing they had over $200k invested in stocks.

Carrol just wanted to move on. She had already told her daughter that she was pregnant with another man's baby. It had been nearly six months since she had seen Baby. The number that she had on him was disconnected. She didn't care that she would have to raise her son by herself. She was just happy to be liberated from her prison of a marriage. "If this is what you want, go ahead. Just remember this is what you asked for!" Greg said as he stormed out of the house. He got into his department issued car, furious.

When he got back down to the homicide building, Tina Jefferies, his African American partner, knew that something was bothering him. "Want to talk about it?" She asked, as they walked to his car to begin their day. Greg sighed as he got into the driver seat. "She knows about us Tina, and she wants a divorce." He left out the part that she was pregnant by another man. He had only learned it himself that morning. "Isn't that what you wanted Greg?" Tina said. "Now we don't have to hide our relationship anymore. I guess you'll be moving in with me after all? And I might as well tell you this now... I'm pregnant."

Greg turned to face her, as his mouth hung open in shock. Tina reached over and lifted his chin up smiling. "I've known for three weeks. I've been debating getting an abortion but since you're getting a divorce now, I can keep my baby." She said with a grin.

***

"You sure my nigga?" Dae Dae asked for the hundredth time. "Come on man! Why you keep asking me am I sure? I told you either you in or not?" Wayne said in an agitated tone. "Hell yeah I'm in." Dae Dae replied. "Aight, they going bowling tonight. We gon snatch them coming out." Wayne said. He saw the look Dae Dae was giving him. "My people gon be with them. Like on the double date they gon let us know when they leaving. We gon have Gudda put the money in the back seat of a car we park under the bridge off Ridgeway, that way we can watch him and see if he try some slick shit feel me?" Dae Dae was mentally inspecting Wayne's plan, and it was a good plan.

Gudda was over one of his female friend's house, getting ready to give her the business when his cell phone started ringing. It was his sister calling him. "What sis?" He answered annoyed.

"Gudda they said they gon kill me if you don't give them

$250,000 dollars!" Kara said in a terrified tone. All the air left

Gudda's lungs. "You got 20 minutes nigga, and if you try any

slick shit your sister dead!" An unknown man spat. "Do you

hear me bitch ass nigga? Think it's a game! I'm a call back in 20

minutes you better have that paper." The call ended. Gudda

stared at his phone for a few seconds then jumped to his feet. He

ran out of the house, leaving his action for the night clueless as

to why. He called his mother as he drove to her new house on

the outskirts of the city.

Vivica was getting ready for bed. She had to get up early and

get on the highway to make the visit to see Abdul, but her son

called her telling her Kara had been kidnapped.

"What I tell you nigga?" Wayne said, looking at Dae Dae. They

had Eli's brother and Gudda's sister zip tied in the back of a

stolen van, two blocks from where they instructed Gudda to

drop the money. They watched Gudda make the drop and pull

off. They then went and retrieved the money.

Dae Dae had Maryln waiting for him at the spot, where they were going to switch cars to kill Wayne and the two of them were going to split the money. Wayne purposely let Dae Dae pick up the bag and check the money as they walked back to his car. Dae Dae thought about the $125k take that he was about to get. He laughed to himself as he thought about the cross he was about to put on Wayne. "What's that?!" Wayne said suddenly in a surprised tone. Dae Dae stopped and looked around. Boom! Wayne hit him in the back of the head with his .38 snub that he had up his sleeve. Dae Dae dropped face first to the cold pavement. Wayne picked up the bag and trotted off to his car.

Chapter XII

Slime was happy to be out of Tennessee, but what he was really delighted about was having some real weed. LJ and Baby had drove down to Tennessee to pick him up, then they drove to Atlanta. When they pulled into the long driveway to the 3,000 square foot colonial style house, LJ and Slime were speechless. "This some real live player shit. Why we ain't been coming down here?" Slime asked. Baby shrugged his shoulders. Only the living room and his bedroom were furnished. "You need to get some more furniture in this bitch. This can be the honeycomb hide out." Slime suggested. Baby nor LJ told him that Fred would be joining them in a few days. "We need some hoes up in this bitch!" Slime rambled on. "Relax nigga. You need to be focusing on what you gon do about yo legal problems." LJ told him. "Ain't nothing to think about! When they catch me I'll worry about that shit. Until then, I'm a live everyday like it's my last. Long as I get to see my daughter and hold her, it is what it is. Till then, I'm bout to fuck Atlanta up!" Slime said grinning. Baby called Julius and told him he was in Atlanta and needed to meet with him. He also got Stacy's number and gave her a call. While they waited for Stacy to get there, they had a session. They smoked a whole box of rellos. When Stacy arrived, she was happy to see Baby, then she noticed the scar running down the side of his face. "What happened to you? You messing up that handsome face like that." "It's a long story." He told her. "Aye, you got any friends or cousins or some females you can call up?" Slime rudely interrupted. "Nah, I ain't that type of girl. But y'all can come to the club tonight and I'm sure you can find what you looking for." She said and turned back to baby. "I was in a bad car accident. I was in a coma for a little while. I lost that phone and couldn't remember your number, Julius just gave it to me." Baby told her. They talked for a little while then they decided to go to Lenox Mall and get fly for the club that night. The last time that Baby was in the strip club that Stacy's father owned, he was iced out looking like a baller. This time he was Plain John. He scanned the club, checking out all the heavily iced-out ballers. When he saw Julius walking through dolo, like he always did, he just smiled.

They had a small booth in the club, so when Baby waved to Julius he walked over to where they were posted up. "What's up my nigga?" Baby said giving him dap. "I'm good. What's up with you? Last I heard you was in a coma?" Julius could see the scar on Baby's face, so he knew that what his sister had said was true. "I'm Steven Segal out this bitch. "Hard To Kill", you hear me?!" Baby laughed, then in a split second the smile vanished. "But on some real shit, while I was in a coma a lot of shit happened that fucked me up. I know I still owe you almost a dollar and a half. I lost everything my nigga I need to smack something." Baby explained. "What do you mean?" Julius asked, playing dumb. "I know you got somebody who, let's just say, you don't too much care for, that I can sting?" Baby said. The two men just stared each other in the eyes. Baby was just talking. He already had a play in the making. Wise had Jazzy drive a trunk full of money up to a house that he had in New York. He was just waiting for the next time and it was on. "I just may have something for you." Julius said, then began telling Baby about some other Mexicans he used to run with that crossed him. LJ saw Julius and Baby huddled up discussing something that looked to be important, so he tapped Slime and told him to walk with him. When Baby heard Julius say that the lick was worth at least 1-2 million dollars, he sat up straight. Baby was no longer interested in getting laid, all he thought about was… Where these mufuckaz at?!

The next afternoon….

Julius pulled in the parking lot of a Mexican restaurant in Cobb County, Baby was in the passenger seat. "It's always the same two dudes sitting in there all day. A tall dark-skinned Mexican, and a short lighter skinned one. They hold the money here until the end of the month when they get more stock in, then they move the money. Like I said, it's at least 1-2 million cash in there at the end of the month." Julius said. Baby scanned the parking lot. "Around back is where you'll have to have a driver waiting with a van, and load that bitch up. The whole key to the lick is getting up in there and getting in position." Julius said. "I'll figure it out, trust me. For 1 to 2 million, ain't no doubt about it." Baby assured him.

For three days Baby sat in the house, smoking blunt after blunt, thinking of a way to pull off the robbery without getting killed. The restaurant wasn't that big but that wasn't the problem. He was laying in his bed staring up at the ceiling when it hit him. "Go through the roof!" He called Julius and woke him out of his sleep. "I got it!" He told Julius excitedly. "I'm on my way over there," Julius said. It took Julius almost an hour to get there. Baby was sitting in the living room by himself when Julius knocked on the front door at 2:30 in the morning. Julius walked in smoking a blunt of his own. "This better be good. You woke me up!" Julius said. "You can sleep later, right now we gotta get this money." Baby told him. Julius sat down on the couch. "All I need is for you to get the power to the restaurant turned off for like an hour. And we need some electric saws. We going through the roof." Baby told him, looking him in his eyes. Julius just smiled at him. "Fuck you smiling for?" Baby knew his smile could only mean one thing. Julius never told Baby that the establishment they were robbing used to belong to him. A shipment of weed from Mexico that he was responsible for got jacked to pay the people who sent it. He gave up the restaurant and close to a million in cash. He suspected his ex-partner was somehow responsible for the shipment that got jacked. The same ex-partner was now using the restaurant the same way he once used it, and now Julius was buying weed from him.

"Look sweetheart, I really need you on this one." He said. "Please Julius, only time I see you is when you need me to do some illegal shit like keep yo electricity on at that restaurant under a bogus ass name. Every time I fuck wit you I'm putting my freedom on the line." Maria snapped. "Didn't I buy you that new Mercedes? Didn't I help you pay off your mortgage? What about our trip to Paris?" Julius said with pleading eyes. Maria knew Julius wanted her to do something crazy, and in the end she would give in to him like she always did. She began speaking rapidly in Spanish. Julius smiled knowing he had her. "We got an hour." Julius told Baby, as they sat in his living room. "The restaurant opens at 11:00am, they get there around 10:00. We need to be inside by 9:00." Julius had all the power tools they would need to get through the roof laying out on the floor in front of them. Thomas Hernandez arrived at A Taste of Mexico like he did on any other day.

As usual, his two-man security team was waiting in the parking lot, making sure that he was safe. The big, taller Mexican walked to the rear of the restaurant and took the large pad lock and thick chain off the freezer. Baby and LJ had been waiting for over an hour for this very moment. As soon as the freezer door opened, Baby slid out of the utilities closet and LJ came out of the staff restroom. Baby hit the big Mexican with the tazer and LJ quickly zip tied his wrist and ankles, then he taped his mouth shut. They canned the big Mexican in the office and went back to their hiding places. After 10 minutes, the second Mexican came looking for his partner and met the same fate that his partner did. It was too easy. One by one all three Mexicans were zip tied and laid down in the office. Baby snatched the computer, hard drive, and surveillance equipment. LJ was waiting for him in the freezer. Julius said 1-2 million dollars, but what LJ saw in front of him made his guts start bubbling.

Saran wrapped kilos of something were stacked almost as tall as him. It had to be at least 300 kilos. When Baby walked into the freezer and saw what LJ was staring at, he looked at LJ and started laughing. They had to get Slime to help them transfer the dope from the freezer to the van. It wasn't until they began transferring the dope that they came across a pallet of more money than any of them had ever seen in their lives. 1-2 million was an understatement. Julius paced Baby's living room floor nervously. He never expected to take 200 kilos of cocaine and 147 kilos of heroine. They hadn't even counted the money yet. "What the fuck you so nervous for?" Baby asked Julius. Julius knew he had fucked up. This was bad. "They're going to kill us all." Julius said. "Who the fuck gon kill us? How they gon know you did it? They gone think some blacks were behind it. "They heard our voices, that was part of the plan. You starting to make us nervous Julius." Slime said. LJ gave Baby a look like "we gotta kill this nigga." "Yo boy buggin on some real shit." Slime said. "We gotta kill Maria, she's the only person that can involve me." Julius said, talking to himself. "Just tell me where the bitch live at, I'll shoot the bitch myself, you trippin my dude, we rich!"

Slime told him. Julius knew things they didn't, like who the money and dope really belonged to. And, the lengths they would go to reclaim what was taken from them.

This was too much. Julius never imagined that the Sanchez brothers had stepped up in the game and started dealing in cocaine and heroin. He was on the brink of having a full-fledged panic attack. "We have to take it back," Julius blurted out. Slime gave Baby a funny look. "Listen to me Baby! We have to take it back!" Julius said, grabbing him by the shoulders. "Man! You trippin', cause we ain't taking shit back! You said Maria's the only one that can connect you to the robbery, right? Slime, go with him and take care of Maria!" Baby ordered. "My pleasure..." Slime said. "LJ, we gotta start counting dis money." Baby said, keeping everything in motion. The plastic wrapped block of money was almost 5 feet high and 3 feet wide. "Listen to me Julius, everything gon be good as long as you don't get paranoid and spooked. Go on with your life as you normally do." Baby handed him the blunt, attempting to calm his nerves. He was about to say something else when his phone rang. It was his cousin China. "Let me take this call y'all." Baby said as he walked off to the kitchen. LJ looked at Slime. Slime told Julius, "Let's go."

"What's up cuz?" Baby said, answering China's call. "Baby why you ain't called Frankie yet? She been calling me, blowing my phone up! Call her damn." "My bad cuz, I'm about to call her right now." Baby promised her. He ended the call with China and called Frankie. "Hello." Frankie answered. "What's up Sis, this Baby." "I been trying to call you boy." She said. "What's up?" Baby asked. "Where you at? I'm not trying to talk over the phone, I got a message from Mel." Frankie responded. "Unless you trying to come to Atlanta you gon have to wait for a minute." He told her. "How long is a minute Baby?" She asked, knowing that time was of the essence. "I don't know, a month, maybe two months." He answered. "It's important Baby," she said, growing impatient. "Well catch a flight down here, I'll pay for it." Baby suggested. "Boy I don't need you to pay for my flight! But since you offering, I'm coming next Friday when I get off work." She said. "Aight cool, I'll see you then, bye." Baby said hanging up. "Bye," said Frankie. Baby walked out of the kitchen to an empty living room. "LJ!" He yelled. When LJ didn't answer he walked up the stairs and called his name again thinking he was in the bathroom. When he still didn't answer he figured that LJ must have left out with Slime.

He walked back down the stairs and went to work on the money. After cutting the plastic wrapper off he took a block of hundred-dollar bills also wrapped in plastic. He peeled the plastic off and saw that it was ten, $10,000 dollar bundles in the block. He began going through the process of removing the $10,000 dollar blocks of money. When he got to the 50th one and it was still over half the block left he knew they had hit the lick of a lifetime. Now he understood why Julius was so scared. He stopped counting the money and sat on the couch thinking about the robbery they had just committed. Julius knew more about the people that they had robbed than he had told them. This kind of money laying around had to belong to a cartel. That was why Julius was so scared. Baby began to contemplate how much they could trust Julius. Julius was the only one that could connect them to the robbery.

"Damn Julius," he said to himself. "Man don't make me have to do this my nigga!" But the more he thought about it, Baby knew what he was supposed to do. But could he do it? Jazzy loved her brother. He sat on the couch wrestling with his conscious as he waited for Julius, Slime, and LJ's return. The strong marijuana he smoked, like cigarettes, finally took their toll on him and he dozed off on the couch. Baby woke up 3 hours later, still alone. He grabbed his cell phone and saw that he had several missed calls. 2 from Stacy, 3 from Jazzy, and 2 from Fred. He remembered Fred was supposed to be on his way down there, so he called Fred back while walking up the stairs to the bathroom. "Yo man, why you ain't been answering yo fuckin phone?! I'll be Downtown, Atlanta tomorrow!" Fred said, in an excited tone. "Aight fool, call me when you a half hour away so I can meet you." Baby said. "Aight fool." Fred said as he hung up. He was on the toilet when he called Jazzy back. "What's up baby girl?" He said. "Baby girl my ass, why da fuck you ain't been answering your phone?! Something could be wrong." She screamed at him. Baby just laughed. "Shut yo crazy ass up. I was in a kush coma. I miss yo crazy ass foreal. When this shit all over with I'm a put a big block of ice on your finger." Baby said with a grin. "Boy don't be trying to gas me up. And don't be saying nothing you don't mean either," Jazzy pouted. "I don't lie to you no more, we passed that. You my ride or die so I ain't gotta lie to you about shit." Baby knew all the right things to say to Jazzy. He manipulated her love for him at will.

"Well, this weekend he wants me to go to Atlanta and make a run for him." Jazzy told him. "Oh yea? He going to re-up?" Baby asked. "I think so." Jazzy answered him. "I'm a meet you in Atlanta this weekend then." Baby said. "Don't play with me Antwan. I miss you." Jazzy whined. "You miss daddy don't you baby?" Baby teased. "Yea." She pouted. "I'm a see you this weekend. I promise, okay?" Baby said. "I love you." Jazzy responded. "I love you more." He responded. "You better nigga, bye." She said hanging up. Baby finished up dropping his number two and headed back downstairs. When he got down there LJ and Slime were there, sitting on the couch. "Where Julius at?" He asked them. Slime looked over at LJ. "Lil bruh... listen to me before you react." LJ started off. "Naw man...what da fuck did y'all do?" Baby shouted, trying not to think of what he knew they had done. "You see how he was acting bruh! It had to be done. We took care of him and the bitch. Now nobody knows what happened but us three." LJ could see it in Baby's eyes that he was crushed. "Da fuck did y'all do! Fuck!" Baby said as he flipped over the coffee table. LJ and Slime just let him have his moment. Eventually he just walked up the stairs to his bedroom. This was going to crush Jazzy, he just knew it. Julius was her only sibling. He could never let her know that he had anything to do with Julius's death.

Chapter XIII

There was nothing that Baby could do to ease the pain that Jazzy was in. It began to weigh heavy on his heart too, because he knew his obsession with money had led to the death of her brother. He wished that he had never brought up his financial problems in the club that night. The night that Julius told him that he had a lick for him. In the days leading up to Julius's funeral, Baby got to meet relatives of their father's, as well as Julius's mother. The two families seemed to be segregated Baby noticed. Julius had two other sisters and a brother all younger than he was. Jazzy spent most of the time there with them.

Everyone looked at him curiously. He felt like the only white guy at a hood barbeque. "Aye yo, why don't you spend some time with your family and we'll link up afterwards." Baby said, after pulling Jazzy off to the side after the burial. "You can't leave me here alone. Don't mind them." She responded. "Come on pretty girl... you need to be with them. I'm not trying to be the cause of any BS because I'm strapped and I ain't going. So let me respect your brother's family. You know I love you Jazzy." He kissed her on her nose, something he always did when he was feeling romantic. Jazzy wrapped her arms around his neck and started sobbing, causing everyone to look in their direction. Baby did his best to console her. "It's gon be alright." He told her while rubbing her back.

"Man I feel foul bruh. Knowing I played a part in Julius's death, then looking her in the eyes and lying. That's some cold shit. What type of nigga can do that and sleep good at night?!" Baby said. "Me." Slime answered him with a straight face. "We came up on 10 million dollars nigga, plus a shit load of work! Julius was just a casualty. It's fucked up, but that's life. You see how he was acting. You rather feel the way you feel now or be sitting in a cell with a "L" talking bout 'I should've killed that nigga' or worse, all of us be dead because he thought we was just gon get some small shit. Hell we ain't make that nigga turn us on to the lick! He offered that shit, so he initiated the whole play. I don't feel sorry. I don't regret nothing. Nigga we rich! Fuck them Mexicans, we can buy hella guns now! This shit we been dreaming about our whole lives. Niggas a kill they mama for 10 million. It was him or us and I chose him flat out."

"I got O.J. money. Fuck them lil niggas and whoever sent em!" Slime ranted. Baby knew Slime was referring to Fred, which was why he hadn't told him Fred was also in Atlanta. 'We gon go out tonight and have a ball. Use some of that money to plush this big ass house out. How much you pay for this Baby?" Slime asked. "300, but it wasn't all at one time. I put down 75 and kept chipping away at it using the money I was getting off the weed Julius was dumping on me." Baby explained. "This a bad mufucka. We gon turn this bitch into the black Playboy Mansion." Slime said with a smile.

Jazzy had never met her uncle Arturo. Arturo was her father's

youngest brother. She didn't know anything about her uncle,

except that he lived in Mexico and rarely came to the states.

"Jasmine, my beautiful niece." Her uncle said with a smile, but

his eyes weren't smiling. He kissed her on both cheeks then held

her by her shoulders. "So that was your boyfriend? Is he the

father of your child?" He asked. "Yes Uncle." Jazzy responded,

feeling uncomfortable in his presence. "When was the last time

that you saw Julius?" He asked. His dark eyes were like staring

into the devil's eyes. She couldn't see anything in them. "It's

been a little while, but I talked to him a few months ago. Why

Uncle?" She answered and queried him. "Because your father

asked me to find out who killed his only living son. You do know

you had another brother who died many years ago aye?" He

asked. This was something that she didn't know, and her uncle

knew that she didn't. "No one will spill Garcia blood and not

answer for it. It's time you learn where you come from. Your

father also asked me to take you back to Mexico until we get to the bottom of who killed Julius." He told her. "I'm not going to Mexico are you crazy?" Jazzy shouted.

"It is not a request. Don't worry about packing, you can buy everything once we get there." Her Uncle stated, firmly. "Maybe you didn't hear me, I'm not going to no damn Mexico!" Jazzy stated adamantly. "Maybe you didn't hear me. You don't have a choice!" Arturo pulled out a cell phone and dialed a number.

Jazzy looked over and locked eyes with the mother of her brother's children. Julius had left two sons behind. Her heart sank even further for her nephews. "Auisale a Hugo que me marque que es urjente." Arturo said into the phone in rapid Spanish then held the phone while waiting for Hugo to call him back. Even while being locked up in a federal prison, Hugo Garcia was still a very powerful man. Something that Jazzy knew nothing about. Arturo's cell phone rang and he answered it while staring Jazzy in the eyes. "Estoy can Jazzy pero ella insiste que no quiere uenir can migo." Arturo nodded his head. "Si." he said, then held the phone out to Jazzy. Not believing he was actually talking to her father, Jazzy snatched the phone out of his hand. "Who is this?' She demanded. If her father had a phone she knew she would have the phone number. "Hola me hermosa Flor nesecito que vallas con tut io es por tu propia proteccion. Porque me contaste que estavas embarasada? Tu tio tetraera a verme pronto pero te estoy protejiendo de hombres malos Jasmine." "Hello my beautiful flower. I need you to go with your Uncle Arturo, it's for your own protection. Why didn't you tell me you were pregnant? Your uncle will bring you to see me soon, but I'm trying to protect you from dangerous men Jasmine." Jazzy began crying. "Padre en que andas? Porque nesesito proteccion? Quien mata a Julio?" Jazzy said, speaking to her father in Spanish. She asked him "What was going on and why did she need to be protected, and who killed Julius?" "No te preocupes te lo explicane todo cuando me vengas a uer por ahorita me te can Arturo. Te amo Jasmin." "I will explain everything to you when you come to see me, now go with Arturo. I love you Jasmine." Jazzy tried to explain to her father that she was with Baby, but he wasn't trying to hear anything else. Hugo Garcia had one thing on his mind, and that was protecting his daughter. She realized that she couldn't win with her father. She handed her uncle back the phone and walked away from him. She ended up in the bathroom where she called Baby. "Baby you have to come and get me, they trying to take me to Mexico." Jazzy said nervously into the phone. "Who trying to make you go to Mexico? What you talking about Jazzy?" Baby said, trying to figure out what was going on. "Please Baby, just come and get me." She said, beginning to cry again. Hearing her sound so distraught made Baby stop the car and bust a U-turn. He raced back to Julius's house. Julius's mother was a very pretty woman, even in her early 40s.

She saw the uncomfortable position Jasmine was in and came to her aid. "Arturo, let me talk to her." The woman said. Jazzy had always liked Tamara, so she went with her away from everyone else so that they could talk in private. Tamara had once been named *Miss Arizona* in the *Miss America Pageant*. She was dressed in an all black Chanel 2-piece suit, with her long black hair pulled back into a ponytail. She had huge solitaire diamonds on her fingers and in her ears. One would label her as a woman of wealth, and they would be correct. She grabbed Jasmine by her hands. "Listen to me Jasmine, I know you don't understand what's going on right now and you're scared but right now, the way I know your father, all he's thinking of is protecting you. I see a lot of myself in you. When your father swept me off my feet with his charm, like you, I didn't understand what I was involved with until I was kidnapped while I was five months pregnant with Julius. The reason that your father kept you and Julius away from the rest of his family for all these years is because of the lifestyle that he can't get out of. He was born into the drug trafficking life. His father and uncles were traffickers Jasmine. After I was released from my captives, I left your father and moved to Canada. Your father got sentenced to 25 years because he was the head of a drug cartel, and now his enemies have finally caught back up with him after all these years. You lost your brother because your father was responsible for, God knows how many, mothers burying their sons and daughters. At the time that I was kidnapped I had thought I was his fiancé, but your father already had a wife and son in Chihuahua, Mexico. They were both killed." Tamara held her hands tight as she continued speaking. "Go with Arturo, Jasmine, it's safer for you. I don't know how they found Julius, but if they found him, we must assume they have found you as well." Jazzy had so many questions to ask her. "He told me that I was going to see him?" It hadn't registered in her mind that when her father first told her that he would talk to her when she came to see him, that it would be in prison. She had never visited her father before. As far back as she could remember, they had always talked on the phone. "He wants to be the one to tell you who he is." Tamara told her while looking into her eyes. Tamara felt so sorry for the girl. She knew her life would never be the same. "Jazzy! Jazzy! Where you at?!" Jazzy heard Baby yelling from inside the house. She took off back into the house towards the sound of his voice.

When Jazzy got to the living room Baby had his gun pointed in her uncle's face, and almost every other male in the room had guns pointed at him. Jazzy instantly placed herself in front of Baby. "Put the gun down Baby, they're not going to shoot." She told him with watery eyes. "What the fuck is going on Jazzy?!"

Baby asked, with his gun still aimed at her uncle's face. "I have

to go with my Uncle Arturo…" she said. "Go where?! Fuck you

mean you gotta go? What about the baby? You ain't about to go

off without me and take my child!" Baby snapped. "Someone's

trying to kill me and I'm going away for my own protection."

Jazzy told him as tears spilled from her eyes. She grabbed his

wrist and lowered his arm. "I can protect you. You ain't gotta go

nowhere fuck that!" Baby said. "I promise you baby, I swear

everything will be ok you don't have to go nowhere, trust me."

Baby's eyes began to water, and it frustrated him because he

couldn't understand what was going on… At that very moment

he realized what it was… he loved Jazzy. "I need you Jazzy.

You can't just leave me and take my son with you." He pleaded.

"I need to go and figure out what's going on. The people who

killed Julius are enemies of my father. I don't know that much

right now but I promise you I will be back. you know I love you

Baby." She kissed him long and hard, both of their tears spilling

down their lips into each other's mouths. Tamara watched in

admiration, as well as sympathy. She knew she was seeing real

love in the young man that Jasmine was in love with. He was

ready to lose his life to protect her. There was something she had to talk to Hugo about. Baby was torn inside. He couldn't tell Jazzy that she had nothing to worry about because LJ and Slime had been the ones that killed her brother. All he could do was hold on to her. He had lost Lisa and his daughter Queen, his mother was somewhere strung out, Low was dead, Kelvin was dead… This was not the life that he envisioned. This is not what he thought the top would be like. "You don't have to go, I got you. Trust me." Baby continued pleading with her. "I have to see my father. I need answers that only he can give me. As soon as I'm done, I'll be back." Baby looked her uncle in his eyes. "If anything happens to her, I'm holding you responsible!" Arturo smiled at him. He admired the young black kids' courage and the love that he had for his niece. Jasmine was the only reason that he would be allowed to walk out of there that day. The next day Jazzy was in Chihuahua, Mexico.

When she stepped out of the black SVU she glanced around the compound that her family lived on in the countryside of Chihuahua. There were four smaller buildings and one large building that sat in the center of the compound. "Come, you need to meet your grandmother. She's waiting for you." Arturo told her, as he escorted her towards the main house. The Spanish style buildings were something Jazzy had never seen before. They found the little old woman in the kitchen. When they entered the kitchen, she immediately stopped what she was doing and ran to Jazzy and wrapped her arms around her as tears flooded her eyes. Salina was delighted to see her granddaughter in person for the first time. Jazzy didn't know what to say to the woman. "Final monte nos reunimos." Finally we meet," Salina said. "Tueves mi abuela?" "You're my grandmother," Jazzy asked. "Si yo soy. Yo soy Salinas Gomez mama de Hugo Gomez." Jazzy could see happiness and sadness in the old woman's eyes. Salina sat her down at the kitchen table and began telling her about her family.

Chapter XIV

LJ felt for his brother. He had never seen Baby in such a depressed state. Although he believed what they did to Julius was necessary and had no regrets, he wished there could have been some other remedy for the situation. Baby stayed to himself, he didn't go out to the clubs with them or partake in the orgies that Slime seemed to always have going on at the house.

After furnishing the house with expensive furniture and flat screen TVs, plus four low key slider cars to get around in, Baby put the rest of the money up somewhere safe. He had Ashley stash $2 million of it for him in a house that he had her by that only the two of them knew of. The rest he had Stacy put in safety deposit boxes. With their money stashed in safety deposit boxes in four different banks all that was left to do was sell the dope they were sitting on. Baby was sitting in his bedroom thinking about Jazzy, who he hadn't seen or talked to in a week. He was so distracted with thoughts of her that he'd forgotten all about Frankie coming to Atlanta until his cell phone rang. "Hello?" He answered. "Boy where you at?! I'm already down here, China and Peaches with me too." Frankie said. Baby gave her the address and told her what exit to take and ended the call. He decided to take a shower and change the clothes that he had been wearing for the last three days. As he was exiting his room two females were walking down the hall wearing nothing but high heels. He walked right by them as if they weren't even there. He locked himself in the bathroom. Once he was inside, he took a long hot shower. As he was coming out of the bathroom, wearing only a towel, he stopped by one of the females he passed in the hall on his way to the shower. "Why you always in your room?" She asked. As he stared at her, he realized her face was very pretty but he couldn't help but stare at her perky breasts that sat up perfectly. She had a flat stomach, a small waist, and thick legs. Her hips seemed to belong on another body. What she lacked in breast, she made up down bottom. She was short and compact. "I'm not really into the wild stuff," he answered her and started walking toward his room. Instead of stopping at the door she followed him into the room. Baby knew that he could fuck her, but he didn't. Instead, he dropped his towel and began getting his self together as if she wasn't even there.

"Aye, you mind lotioning my back please?" Baby asked nonchalantly. "What happened to you? All these scars, it look like they hurt." She asked. "You talk funny, where you from?" Baby asked her. She smiled and responded, "I was born and raised in Atlanta, GA. I'm from Summerhill… And just because I like walking around naked don't mean I'm a stripper or prostitute, cause I'm not." "What school you go to?" He asked, as he sat on the edge of the bed in his boxers. She climbed behind him to apply the lotion to his back as she responded. "I go to Spellman. I'm majoring in Criminal Psychology." "All that's good, but who are you?" He asked, not knowing her name. "My name is Savannah. And your name is Baby. You the Birdman too? Flying in any weather?" She asked smiling. After Savannah finished putting the lotion on his back, Baby pulled out an all white, Prada jogging suit, and the matching white low cut Prada sneakers to complete his look. "You look good in that." Savannah said, complimenting him. "Well you need to put on some clothes," he responded to her compliment. "Why? You intimidated by my flesh? Why you ain't down there with your friends having fun?" She caught him off guard with that. Thinking about what she said he could understand why. Normally, he would be downstairs with Slime, LJ, and Fred having a ball. "Honestly, I don't know. I guess I done had enough fun," he reasoned out loud. "Don't be too hard on yourself, the stuff they doing downstairs I'm not into either. I just want to lay out in the sun and chill." She said. At that moment, something that China told him came to his mind and he just started laughing. "What's so funny?" Savannah asked. "Nothing its cool, inside joke." Baby responded. When Savannah walked out of his room, he stood in front of the mirror on his dresser, looking at his reflection. "Don't let the game turn you bad Antwan, you're a good person." He heard his mother telling him.

What he saw in the mirror wasn't a good person though. The good die young like Kelvin, like Low, like Julius, like Rick. All his brushes with death he had survived, and why? He stared into his own eyes and came face to face with the answer. "I'm a bad person." He told his reflection. LJ, Slime, and Fred, were sitting under beach umbrellas beside the pool smoking and drinking, enjoying the Georgia sun and beautiful women running around naked. There were at least a dozen women there.

Some were in the pool, others were lounging around doing the same thing LJ, Slime, and Fred, were doing. When Fred and Slime first saw each other LJ and Baby had to get in between them, now they were acting as if nothing ever happened.

Savannah was on her way back upstairs after she had showered

and gotten dressed when the doorbell rang. Seeing that there

was no one there to answer the door she took the liberty of

playing door girl. When she opened the door China, Peaches,

and Frankie stood there. "Is Baby here?" China asked. "Yeah,

he upstairs in his room." Savannah answered. China entered

the house followed by Peaches and Frankie. "It sounds like

they're having a party." Peaches said. "Everybody else out

back." Savannah told them, thinking they were just three more

pretty faces there to get high, drunk, and whatever else they

wanted to do. She led them outside to the pool. When they got

out there and saw all the naked girls, they just looked at each

other in disbelief. It was Fred who called out to them first. When

LJ and Slime saw them, they stood up. "Slime was iced out,

both wrists, his neck, and his ears. He spent $300k on jewelry

alone, in two days at three different jewelry stores in Downtown,

Atlanta. "Girl they is doing entirely too much!" Peaches said.

They had all seen Slime's face on the news several times, and

here he was looking like he didn't have a care in the world.

"Whose house is this?" Was the first thing China asked them.

"This lil bruh house." Slime answered, staring Peaches in the eyes. He had always had a thing for her. "Where Baby room at?!" China asked, then headed back into the house. Savannah had already gone upstairs to get him, so when they entered the house Baby was walking down the stairs. Seeing China instantly put a smile on his face. "What's up with my favorite cousin?" He asked playfully. Frankie and Peaches were sizing Savannah up as she stood beside Baby. "Yall want something to drink?" Baby asked them, pausing on the stairs. "Where da weed at niggah?!" Frankie asked. "Let's go up to my room, I don't really be down here that much." Baby told them. They followed him upstairs to his bedroom, which was more like a studio apartment. "Baby whose house is this for real??" China asked. "Mine. I bought it before my accident. I had it close to a year almost." Baby said chuckling. China couldn't believe her 17 year old cousin bought a house that was twice the size as hers. Baby walked to his dresser and grabbed a crystal candy container filled with weed. "Who is this?" Frankie asked, referring to Savannah.

"Oh, this is my friend, Savannah. Savannah, this my cousin China and this her friend Peaches and that's Frankie." Baby said. Peaches didn't waste any time rolling up a stupid fat blunt, then she began talking, like she always did. "You heard about Dae Dae?" she asked Baby. "Naw... What about him?" Baby responded, curiously. "Somebody shot him in the head. Somebody must have been praying for him cause he didn't die. It was a shootout at Celebrities, the Carplin and Ridgeway boys got into it with some Downtown niggaz and some innocent girl got killed. It's been mass shootings in Avondale doe." Peaches said, rambling. None of what she said mattered to Baby. "Anybody seen my mother?" he asked, looking from face to face, hoping to see a sign that one of them had seen her. One by one they said "no." "I talked to Lisa tho..." China told him. "What she was talking about?" Baby asked. "She asked how you were doing, she told me she was doing okay, and she said Queen getting big. You need to go be with your daughter, even if you and Lisa not together. At least be in the same city. All the shit you've been through in Cincinnati. Getting shot, shot at, all the crazy shit you involved in, you need to just get away and start over." China was really concerned about her cousin. She knew he wasn't your average hood nigga. He was 17 years old with a house that couples that worked 20 years couldn't afford to have. "She just up and left me when I was close to dying. I understand why, don't get me wrong, but still…" He said, before China could tear into him. "She knew what type of life I lived." Baby continued. "Baby, that shit ain't normal. Somebody held a gun to your daughter head! I would have done the same thing. This is not a game boy, you need to grow up and realize that." China scolded him. Savannah just sat there listening. She enjoyed reading urban novels when she wasn't studying, and this was a chapter right out of one of them. "Right now I've got a lot on my mind. I understand what you're saying, I really do, and I know you just trying to lookout for me. It's a lot you don't know China and I ain't trying to talk in front of everybody. Just know, I ain't dumb and I'm not the same person I was before my coma." He said, sternly. China could see in his eyes that he wasn't the same person he used to be. "Frankie what was so important you had to come all the way to Atlanta?" He asked her. "Let's give them some privacy." China said. On que Peaches and Savannah followed her to the door. Frankie waited until the door shut behind Peaches to speak.

"Baby, Mel sent me a letter through his lawyer and he told me to tell you that if you take care of what happened to my son, he'll give you his connect." "Frankie if I could take care of it I would. I'm not Superman. Everybody wants me to help them with their problems, but I have problems of my own I need help with." Baby said. Frankie stood up from the couch where she was sitting and walked up on him. "They killed my son baby." She said as her eyes began to fill with tears. Baby could see the pain in them. "Damn she beautiful," he thought. "I lost two of my closest friends too Frankie." He said back. "But you didn't lose your son." She began crying. In an attempt to console her, he wrapped his arms around her and allowed her to seek refuge in his embrace. Frankie felt his manhood swelling in the thin material of the jogging suit that he was wearing. She hadn't been with a man since Mel was arrested, and that was over a year ago. She pressed her body up against his and when she did, she felt his hardening pole poke her in the stomach. Baby looked down into her eyes and neither one of them spoke, yet they had communicated to one another.

"Girl look at all these bitches just running around naked!" China said. "Bitch I wanna strip down and get in that water!" Peaches said. "I bet yo triflin ass do bitch…" China countered. "Bitch don't act like you all goody two shoes because I got memories of your drunk ass in Miami and Atlanta at the freaknik!" Peaches reminded her. "Bitch do what you wanna do, I'm not your mother." China walked away and headed over to where LJ, Slime and Fred were. "What y'all drinking?" She asked. "Some strawberry lemonade with patron, some type of wine, and some other shit. I'ts good doe." LJ assured her. China grabbed the pitcher and a cup and poured herself a drink, she took a sip. "Hmm this is good who made this?" She asked. "Cherry. The girl with the red hair, she a bartender." Slime said. China grabbed several of the rolled blunts that they had sitting in a glass dish and walked over to an empty table and made herself comfortable. She kicked off her shoes and put her sunglasses on and fired up a blunt. "Man, I'm bout to get

Peaches ass!" Slime said, as he got up to go pursue her. LJ and Fred watched him try to shoot his shot.

"Look at China, man I been wanting to fuck her since I first seen her." LJ said with a slur. Usually, he was the reserved and detached one. Since killing Julius, which was his second body, he began drinking and smoking excessively to numb his conscious. He wasn't like Slime. Slime already had two bodies that he was on the run for, so another one was nothing to him. LJ got up and went over and sat at the table with China. Fred decided to join the ladies in the pool. He stripped down butt naked and cannonballed into the deep end, splashing Slime and Peaches. "What is wrong with him?" China asked LJ, as he took a seat at the small table with her. "He just having fun. You know we got extra swimsuits in the house if you wanna get in the water?" "LJ... I know you ain't over here trying to run yo game on me?" China asked with a smile. She was already beginning to feel a buzz from the concoction that she was drinking on. "We young and having fun, I ain't trying to run no game. I don't need to… you know what it is… and I know you don't mess with nothing ass niggas and being that I'm far from that… what's up?" LJ said, laying it all out. "You talking about we young, boy you young… I'm 29 years old, with a son. I ain't got time for games or lames." China said, having fun with him. "You still young, like I said, and as far as the other shit you said I can't even speak on it because I don't know what that is... you know what's up! You see the greatness in front of you." LJ said confidently. "How old are you LJ?" She asked. "I'm 19, why?" He answered. China started laughing. "Because what I want and what you want are two different things. I done had my fun. I ain't looking to have fun no more, I want someone I can be in a committed relationship with. Someone that doesn't mind taking care of me. Who can actually take care of me… I'm not a cheap bitch." "Well I ain't a cheap nigga, and believe me I can take care of you." He said. "Can you?" She asked, enjoying their flirting. "Let me show you better than I can tell you." LJ told her. "The floor is yours big man, show me what you got." She said, teasing him. LJ was dead serious though. China just thought he was playing around.

Savannah wondered what Baby and the girl that he was upstairs

with were doing. "Why would he want her and not me?" She

asked herself. She knew that she wasn't ugly Frankie may have

had a prettier face than her, but she had a better body than

Frankie. When Baby finally came downstairs, he let Frankie

walk down first. He waited before he came down to join them.

China new what Frankie wanted to talk to Baby about, so when

she saw Baby walk outside she excused herself from LJ and

asked Baby could she talk to him. "You better not do that shit.

That's not your problem. You don't need to put yourself in

anymore situations." China said, talking to him like she was his

mother. "I'm not stupid China. Everybody wants something

from me. I know I can't please everyone. Come on tho, we bout

to hit the mall. I'm taking y'all out tonight, on me." Baby said.

"Now that's my kind of talk! You know your friend LJ trying to

holla at me. But I don't do the help." China said, chuckling.

Baby's face frowned up, but he didn't expose LJ's hand. "You

trippin' cuz." He said and walked back outside.

Chapter XV

"Yo quierob todos Muertos todo Que no quede niuno de ellos induyendo a los ninos acabarnos a todo es epinedia unavez y para siempre!" "I want them all dead! Every last one of them, including the children! We end this feud once and for all." Hugo ended the call then walked out of his cell and passed the phone to his holder. Everywhere he went inside USP Hazelton (United States Penitentiary), in West Virginia, he had a dozen men with him ready to put their lives on the line for him at any given moment. Hugo was The Boss not a boss. His feud with the Sanchez family went back to his father and his father's father. The Gomez and Sanchez families were two of the biggest families in Chihuahua, Mexico. After the death of his father and uncle, Hugo tried his best to end the generational feud between the two families. However, when his wife and son were killed, with the help of the Chihuahua Cartel, he murdered almost every male Sanchez. Only sparing the elderly and the children, which came back to haunt him because those children were men now, and just as he did, now they wanted revenge for the deaths of their slain fathers, brothers, and uncles. Losing Julius hurt him, but Hugo was not a man who displayed his emotions for others to see. At the end of a 25 year sentence, his plans were centered around his freedom. For him, walking away from the cartel he built meant death. There was no out for him. His position was the only thing keeping him and his family from being murdered. Backed by the Chihuahua Cartel, he was able to build his own cartel. But it was his slain Colombian wife that put him in position. Her family supplied him with the best cocaine Colombia produced. The cocaine was only part of the reason that the Chihuahua Cartel backed him. His means to get the cocaine from Colombia to Mexico was really why he had the backing of the Chihuahua Cartel. That alone made him too valuable to lose. For 20 years he built his cartel into one that could compete with the Chihuahua Cartel, but instead of cutting his ties and becoming competition to the Chihuahua Cartel he instructed his nieces and female relatives to marry relatives of the Chihuahua Cartel members. With that in place, the Garcia's in the Chihuahua Cartel were bonded by blood.

Together they could compete and even the odds against the mighty Sinaloa and Sonora cartels. The Sanchez family had aligned themselves with the cartel, which meant things were about to get real bloody. Baby walked into the visiting room with his Aunt Lucia at the Hazleton Federal Penitentiary. As he was waiting to be seated, he thought he recognized a light-skinned female with long black straight hair. He felt that he knew her from somewhere but couldn't think of where. His uncle Piere came out with another tall, brown-skin, musclebound, dude with long dreads. Piere, along with the other guy, looked at him then his uncle said something to the guy and headed over to where Baby and his sister were waiting. Piere gave his sister a hug and kiss on the cheek first. Lucia then got up and walked to the vending machine, giving the men some time to talk alone. "You see the guy I was just talking to? He's from West Virginia. We were talking and I told him about Ramon being killed." Baby cut him off, "Unc, I already took care of it. The guy who killed Ramon is dead." Baby told him. Piere stared into his nephew's eyes. "I know that already, but did you know he was set up by the people he went down there with?" Piere saw the look of surprise on his nephew's face.

"That's the way it always happens, it's always someone close to

you that wants your position. Either because they are jealous, or

they feel you just don't deserve it. Ain't no friends in the game.

All we have is family. You see the girl sitting with my boy A1?

That's his sister, you don't remember her?" Piere queried him.

"She looks familiar, but I can't remember from where..." Baby

answered. "You need to tighten up nephew. That's the girl who

set up the guy for you, who killed Ramon." Piere told him. Baby

looked over at her just when her and her brother were looking

at him. Baby realized why he didn't remember her, because the

last time he saw her, her hair was red and short.

"The guy's name is Wise. My boy A1 hooked his boy up, who

you killed, with a plug but the plug ain't moving right now. And

from what I hear, Wise is desperately trying to make a move.

I'm a get him to Atlanta. You just make sure he never leaves

Atlanta." Piere said, looking him in the eyes. When Lucia

returned from the vending machine Piere had said all that he had needed to say, and Baby understood him clearly. Baby caught Keoka staring at him several times.

When she got up to use the restroom, the tight blue jeans she wore gave every inmate in the visiting room something to talk about when they got back to the compound. For the rest of the visit Baby couldn't stop looking over, checking Keoka out. "I'll call you and tell you where you need to be in Atlanta. Give me a couple days." Piere said, then gave him a hug. Baby didn't ask him how he was going to get Wise to Atlanta. "Go ahead Auntie... I'm a catch a ride with my friend." Baby said, as they were leaving the visit. Keoka looked at him like he was crazy as they walked through the lobby of the prison. She didn't think he was serious until he followed her back to her car. "I know you don't think you getting into my car?" Keoka blurted out. "Ok, I know we got off on a bad start but your brother and my uncle on the same team, so you can't be mad at me." Baby said smiling. "You fuckin' killed Black in my house and was about to kill my brother!" Keoka yelled in a hush tone. Baby looked around nervously. "Aye, keep that shit down and open the got damn door!" He said seriously. His tone of authority scared her. She had already seen what he was capable of, and the way her brother talked about him already made her curious. She unlocked the doors and they got into her 5 series BMW. "Look I know you're probably thinking I'm some cold hearted killer, but I'm not. Dude had that coming. Why didn't you tell me Wise set my cousin up?" Baby asked sternly. "I didn't know until that morning. He told me something like, how did I think he knew I was driving dope and money for Ramon? I just want this shit to be over!" She screamed. "Come on let's get out of here and find somewhere that sells real food." Baby said. Instead of protesting she complied and drove to a restaurant not far from the hotel she was staying in. "So how did you meet my cousin?" Baby asked, as they waited on their food. "Same place where I met you… at the club." She answered. "I thought we were starting over." Baby said with a smile. "So, you are human? You smile…" Keoka said, sarcastically. "You too pretty to be so mean. You know that, and you too pretty to be stripping too." Baby told her. Keoka didn't have a quick comeback for that. "Well, welcome to my life. I'm just a country girl from West

Virginia trying to survive in this cold world full of bad people."
She put emphasis on bad people and Baby laughed. "So, I'm a
bad person to you?" He asked. "Hell yea! You're a murderer,
you kill people." She answered him. "Sometimes people need to
be killed. That don't make me a bad person." He rebutted.

"You think you smart, don't you? You got evil eyes. I can see
the devil in you." Keoka said, staring him in his eyes. "Now that
might be true... I'm trying not to let him take my soul. I'm
fighting, fighting with everything I got." Baby told her.
Something in the way that he said it told her that he meant
every word. "Sometimes we gotta do what we gotta do." She
said, looking into his eyes. "Yeah, I know all about it, trust me."
He said. "So how long your brother got, if you don't mind me
asking." He changed the subject. "They gave him 10 years. But
he been gone a little over 4 years. I think he got like three years
left, somewhere around there." She answered. "You miss him,
don't you? I can tell." Baby asked. "How?" Keoka responded.
"The way you kept smiling on the visit. You haven't smiled like
that not one time since then." Baby told her. "Probably because

I'm scared as hell. I don't know if you gon kill me for a reason I don't even know of." She said seriously. "You in good hands with Allstate." Baby said sarcastically. "My uncle said that your brother was his boy, so I don't have no problems with you." Baby continued. She smiled at him. "That's what I'm talking about." Baby said, with a smile of his own.

Chapter XVI

Wise finally got the call that he had been waiting on. Rasta had told him to come to Atlanta. He was running low on work, and due to his almost depleted stash, he had to make his servings smaller. That made his customers upset. They complained, but the quality was still better than everything else out there, so they still copped from his workers. "Yo Science, I need you and Godson to hold things down while I go to Atlanta this weekend." Wise told him. "Who you taking with you God?" Science asked, wanting to go with him. "More than likely Scooter and a few lil niggaz. Gotta call baby mama and see if she gon make the drive for me." Wise said. "If she don't son, you know Jennifer a do it son. She dying to prove herself." Science pointed out to him. Jennifer was a pretty, white chick he was dealing with before he had met Sophia. He had really thought that Sophia was the one. He hadn't seen or heard from her in almost two months though now. One thing he didn't do was stress over a bitch. The mother of his kids was Dominican and drop dead gorgeous, and he didn't break for her. It was his way or the highway. "Matter of fact God, I think we gonna go head and let Jennifer make this run. She can take her sister and her kids." Wise said, liking the idea. He grabbed his cell phone off the table and called Godson. "Yo, peace God. Where you at?" Wise asked him once he answered the phone. "I'm with Scooter. We leaving our spot in the Manor." Godson answered. "I need y'all to come straight here." Wise said. "What's going on? Everything good?" Godson asked skeptically. "Yeah, everything good God, hurry up and get here." Wise answered. "We on our way," Godson told him then hung up. Godson looked over at Scooter as he drove the car. "What he talking about?" Scooter asked. "I don't know." Godson replied, with a worried look on his face. Scooter drove straight to City Park and pulled up in front of the high rise where Wise's spot was. During the last month, Scooter's position in Wise's organization brung him a lot of hate and jealousy from many of his peers, as well as his adversaries. By replacing Black, he was now the enforcer. He was the one making sure that everything ran smooth.

He put a lot of people that he trusted in position to watch his back and he took positions from those that he felt were not playing their positions to their fullest capability. Scooter had never considered himself handsome, however, under the advice of Godson he started using *Proactive,* the face products, for his acne and to his surprise, it was working really well. As they walked towards the high rise, they received stares from the females outside showing off their bodies in the warm summer weather. A few called out their names. "I see you building your fan base God." Godson said with a smirk as they waited on the elevator. "I ain't tripping on these hoes my nigga, I'm focused on this bread." Scooter said, meaning it not just talking like a lot of niggas did. "That's what's up son. You can't allow yourself to be ruled by your lower self. Man is mind. We rule over everything on this earth. Everything submits to us God." Scooter nodded his head in acknowledgement. The two of them had a lot in common which allowed them to relate to one another. When they got to Wise's floor, they noticed the guards on point, as they should be. Godson did his distinctive knock on the door and seconds later Science opened it. "Peace God."

Science greeted them. Godson returned the greeting. When they entered the apartment, Wise was sitting in the living room with Jennifer. "Peace God." Godson said entering the living room. "Peace God." Wise returned the greeting. "What's up boss man?" Scooter asked, as he took a seat on the couch. "We gotta run down to Atlanta this weekend. Godson I'm a have you ride with me. Scooter, you and Science can stay here and hold the fort down. "I got family in Atlanta." Scooter announced. Wise had thought about the idea of having Scooter go with him, but he decided against it. Although he still felt like Godson was harboring ill feelings towards him over him getting Ramon killed, he still rathered have Godson with him. He had already set his back up protection in place just in case Rasta tried any funny business.

"I need you here right now Scooter. I can't afford things to malfunction at this moment. I already got niggaz trying to jump ship. Them Saint Albans niggaz trying to push the dope on people that's already buying from us. I need you to make sure them niggaz don't try no funny shit in my absence. We gotta keep the pressure down. The second we let up we can lose everything." Wise commanded.

"I got you my nigga. You know you can depend on me to keep shit going. I'm a hold it down, believe that my nigga!" Scooter said confidently. Wise smiled. "No doubt son. I trust you." Wise responded. Really Wise didn't trust Scooter at all, which was why he kept him close. What none of them knew was, he had another entire crew of Huntington niggaz that he was feeding. He was also sicking them on his competition. The moment Scooter stepped out of line he would be a dead man. Science was the only person that he felt like he could trust. Like him, Science just wanted the money. He wasn't concerned about anything else. He suspected that Science knew that he played a part in Ramon's murder.

"Jennifer let's go." Wise said, and together they walked out of the apartment. "What's up Science?" Scooter asked, starting a conversation. "Another day, another dollar. I'm all about the money son." Science stated while inhaling on the blunt in his hand. "Yeah I know... I think I know who killed y'all boy."

Scooter said. "Who you talking bout, Black??" Science asked

nonchalantly. "Naw Ramon." Scooter replied. "You know bro

was cool but that was Wise's man for real. I'm down here on the

strength of Wise." Science had suspected that Wise was involved

in Ramon's murder as soon as he heard about Ramon getting

killed. He actually felt that Ramon's death put him in a better

position. With Ramon out of the picture, he had been making

twice as much money than what he was making when Ramon

was alive. Science wasn't stupid, he just didn't broadcast his

thoughts. "What's up son? Who did it?" Science asked, just to

play along. "It was them Saint Alabans niggaz." Scooter replied.

He watched Science, trying to read his reaction. "Well then,

they gon pay for it. You should have said something while Wise

was here." Science said, trying to see where Scooter really was

with Wise. He knew how close Scooter was with Ramon before

he was killed and he didn't trust him. He had told Wise he didn't

trust him, but Wise was already a step ahead of him. "I need to

make a run. I'll get up with y'all later." Scooter said, then gave

them some dap. When he got outside to his car he called his

cousin Tyrone, who was over in Huntington, and told him that he was about to swing through.

Stacy was working the bar, as usual, in her father's club when three Mexicans walked up to the bar and asked to speak to her father. She had never seen any of them before, so she hesitated. "Tell him that friends of Mr. Vargas are here, and he'll want to see us, Stacy." The Mexican said, stone-faced. She didn't ask any questions. She went to the back to get her father. Red was in his office running money through several money machines when Stacy entered. "Daddy it's three Mexicans out there looking for you talking about they friends of Mr. Vargas." Red stopped what he was doing when he heard the name of his old drug supplier. Azael Vargas worked for Ceasar Sanchez. Rumor was Ceasar Sanchez was connected to the Sinaloa Cartel. After serving 12 years on a 15 year sentence, Red came home and went legit. He worked hard to get his credit up. He was determined to keep his word to his daughter and not go back to the streets, though some days he wanted to. There was nothing like having 2-3 million cash you could put your hands on at any given moment. Red wondered why Azael Vargas sent his men to see him after all these years. "Stay here," Red told his daughter. Red got up from his desk and walked over to his wall safe where he retrieved his gun. "Daddy what's going on?" Stacy asked with a worried look on her face. "I don't know but I'm about to find out!" Red was a high yellow brother with freckles and red hair. In his early 50s he was in excellent shape. A product of Bankhead's notorious projects, Bowen Homes, Red wasn't a man that scared easy. He came up with some of the most brutal gangsters and hustlers Atlanta had produced. He stopped and told two of his security personnel to follow him. He spotted three Mexicans sitting at the bar facing the club and walked down on them.

"How can I help you gentlemen?" He asked. "We are here on behalf of Mr. Vargas." One spoke up. "I know that already," Red said cutting him off. "What do you want?" He asked calmly. The same Mexican responded, "Can we go somewhere and talk, just the two of us? My men will stay where they are?"

Red looked at his two security men. "Okay come on." Red said and walked to an empty VIP booth. Stacy didn't know what was going on. She knew that her father had once been heavily involved in the streets but that was all behind him now. He was now a black businessman trying his best to stay clean and do things legally. After the longest 15 minutes of her life her father walked back into the office.

"What did they want Daddy?" Stacy asked impatiently. "That boy who started coming in here with Julius, what do you know about him Stacy?" Red asked his daughter. "What boy?" Stacy asked, uncertain of what her father was talking about. "The one from Cincinnati that I sold the house to, that's who." Her father clarified. "I don't understand. What does he have to do with you?" Stacy asked confused. "Julius was killed and one of their stashes was robbed for 15 million in cash and dope. They were just in here the other night popping bottles. They know Julius has been hanging out with some black guys and one of them has tattoos on his face. I didn't tell them anything but if they know that then somebody knows something and is talking, so that's why I asked you what do you know about him?" Stacy thought about the safety deposit boxes she had gotten for Baby. "They think he killed Julius?" She asked with a look of shock on her face. "Something like that. I'm not trying to be in the middle of no war with them crazy ass Mexicans, so you need to tell your friend to get the hell out of Atlanta!"

Later that evening at the club.........

"I can't remember where he was from but I know he ain't from Atlanta. Like I said, he cool with Stacy." "Do you know if they were sexually involved?" The Jamaican sounding man asked her. Babygirl danced at Stacy's father's club. She had heard about Julius's murder just like everyone else had. So when the Jamaican started asking around about Julius at the club, another dancer told him that she had seen Julius in the last week, before he died, at the club hanging out with some guys. And that one of them had a bunch of tattoos on his face. She had also told him that they were cool with Babygirl, which was why Rasta was now questioning her. Rasta was being supplied by the people who Julius put Baby on to rob. "I appreciate your time."

Rasta said, while handing her 5 hundred dollar bills. "One more thing… is Stacy here right now?" He asked. "Nah she left early." Babygirl answered.

Baby kept his poker face on in front of Stacy. "Look whether you did it or not I'm just trying to give you a heads up. My father said these people are some cartel out of Mexico. If you did do it, I know you ain't gonna to tell me you did it." Stacy said looking into his eyes, trying to look for a tell-tell sign that he was lying. "Look Stacy, Julius was like my brother. I'm just as fucked up about this shit as you. All I did was kick it with him. You know me and his sister used to mess around. Why would I do some shit like that? And $15 million dollars? I'm hustling but I ain't hustling that good!" He told her, lying. "Just leave Atlanta for a while Baby, please!" She pleaded. She didn't have to tell him twice. He had already transferred the dope to a smaller place he was renting in Dallas, GA. China had found it for him. As soon as Stacy left, he went downstairs and told LJ and Slime what Stacy had told him. "How da fuck they know about me?" Slime asked. "They asked around the club more than likely. Asking the dancers who he had been seen there with in the last few weeks before his death." LJ said mad at himself for not foreseeing that. "All I know is we need to go." Baby said. "Go where?" Slime asked. "West Virginia," Baby said. "Who da fuck in West Virginia?" Slime asked. "Don't worry about it... y'all leaving tonight, I'll be right behind y'all." Baby knew he had to take care of the business for his uncle, so he couldn't leave just yet. "Man fuck dem! We can shoot just like they can shoot. I just don't give a fuck! I'm on whatever you on lil bruh." Slime said, meaning every word of it. "Im on staying alive and free. So we gonna hit West Virginia and fuck that up for a minute. I got something already in the making." Baby was trying to look out for the few people he still considered his brothers.

Chapter XVII

Wise checked Godson into his hotel first, then he drove not even

five minutes up the street to the hotel he reserved. Jennifer and

her sister were also staying in the same hotel just on a different

floor. Once he got to his room, he called Jennifer and told her to

come up to his room. The reason that he checked Godson into a

different hotel was to protect the buy money. He had his

younger cousin and a few of his friends at the same hotel that

Godson was at, to make sure he didn't try anything stupid.

Jennifer knocked on the hotel door. He let her in and walked to

the bedroom. Jennifer dropped her luggage and walked to the

bedroom behind him. Jennifer was a black man's kryptonite. A

pretty white girl with big natural breasts and a $10,000 dollar

ass that she paid for, that wasn't too big but was just the right

size for her thick legs. After an hour of sweaty sex, they both

showered and headed out of the hotel room. They hit the

famous Lenox Mall, then Wise took her to a shoe store that a

college friend of his owned Downtown. He had to show her off to his college friends, the same way he had done Sophia. He made plans with his friends for later that night. Atlanta was something like a second home for him. A lot of guys that he had met in college were either successful business owners, in the NBA, or on their way. Even though he was kicked out of school he still became a successful story and had to come back and broadcast it.

***

Baby was zoned out. He had been staying at Savannah's apartment in Downtown, Atlanta. Savannah turned out to be just what he needed. Everything he asked her to do she did. She drove him all over Atlanta. They were currently checked into the same hotel that Wise was checked into, thanks to a heads up from Rasta. Later on that night Wise was supposed to be linking up with Rasta at the strip club. "I need you to put some of this baby oil on my back." Savannah said, walking out of the bathroom naked, smelling like cherry blossom body wash. Seeing Savannah naked was something he had gotten used to.

The girl just didn't wear clothes. As soon as she walked in the house, she got naked.

It was hard to see her not being a stripper. She damn sure had the body for one. She laid on her stomach and Baby squirted baby oil on her back and butt. As Baby massaged the oil into her skin she let out small moans and sighs. When he was finished Savannah got up and just stared at him, seeing the bulge in the front of his sweatpants, she couldn't understand why he wouldn't fuck her. "Are you gay? Be honest, I won't tell nobody." She asked him. Baby just started laughing. "What's so damn funny? You are, ain't you?" She continued. "Why because I won't fuck you? I'm not trying to have you running around here fucked up girl." Baby told her. "Boy! You ain't got it like that, let me see it." Savannah was thirsty and didn't care if he knew it. "Me showing you only gon make you want it even more. We cool, I ain't trying to mess that up. On some real shit my nigga, I like you. You don't fuck with me because of what I got or what I can do for you." He admitted to her. "Just show me and you ain't gotta worry about me doing nothing. We can be naked together and just chill. This is how God created us, what's so wrong with it?" She said, trying to convince him. "So you on some nudist shit huh?" He asked. "I've been to a nudist beach in Miami. I like walking around naked, I feel free. It's not about sex all the time. I just enjoy the human body, it's magnificent how God designed us." She continued. "If I take my clothes off you gon behave yourself? Because I'm packin', working with a monster." He said laughing as he began undressing. When he was completely naked Savannah just stared at him smiling. "You're beautiful. Can I touch it?" She asked, walking up to him and touching his manhood. "Ok now let's go to sleep."

She grabbed his hand and pulled him into the bed where she cuddled up with him. "This bitch crazy." Baby said to himself as he spooned with her.

Godson sat in the hotel room watching the $640k of buy money. His job was to wait for Wise to call and then he would meet Jennifer in the lobby with the money. He was basically babysitting the money. "I can take this shit and just ride off," he thought as he stared at the suitcase full of money. The ring of his cell phone snapped him out of it. "Peace God." He answered the call with a smile. Wise wasn't as smart as he thought he was.

***

Stacy wasn't green to the game so when the light skinned guy with wavy hair and a Jamaican accent began asking about Julius, she knew the Mexicans sent him. Instead of denying seeing Julius with Baby and his friends, she admitted to seeing them. "Do you know where the guys were from?" Rasta asked. "Somewhere in California." Stacy lied. "If you see any of them again give me a call. I will compensate you for your time very generously." Rasta said. "I sure will." Stacy lied to him. She watched Rasta walk to the exit and leave. She went back to the bar. Her father knew she had been talking to the light skin fellow about Julius, so he kept his eyes on her via the video cameras hidden all around the club. Once he saw Stacy return to her station, he hit a few keys on his computer and footage of Baby, Slime, LJ, and Julius sitting in the VIP booth appeared on the screen. Red's gut told him that something had gone wrong between Julius and the three men. He copied the footage onto a disk then erased all the footage he had of them from his computer. He picked up his cell phone and made a call to his nephew.

***

After leaving the Foxhole strip club located in Downtown, Atlanta, Rasta called Wise. "Bredren." He said, when Wise answered the phone. "Peace God. What up with you?" Wise answered. "Me just checking on you trying to see if you okay Bredren." Rasta said in his Jamaican accent.

"I'm good. I'll be leaving out in about an hour or so. Meet me at The Gentlemen's Club Downtown. You know where it is?" Wise asked.

"Yes, me know where it is Bredren. See you there and me will have the best weed waiting for you." He said. "I'll meet you there in a few hours, it's only 9 now." Wise stated. "Okay rude boy." Rasta sad, ending the call. After hanging up the phone he made another call to the guys he had waiting for Stacy to get off work. Next, he called his friend at the Hazelton Federal Penitentiary. "Dem boy feena meet me inna hour bredren.' Rasta informed him. "You call your people and tell him to be outside the hotel." Al wrote down the name of the hotel and the club that Rasta gave him. "Good looking out my nigga. I owe you a favor." Al told him. "Me settle the debt when ya cuma home bredren." Rasta ended the call. Al hung up that call and then dialed the number that Piere had gave him on his nephew. Baby was out cold when Savannah nudged him and told him his cell phone was ringing. The first thing that Baby noticed was how hard his dick was, then how soft Savannah's ass was. His dick was resting right in the crack of her ass. He reached back and grabbed his cell phone off the nightstand. When he seen the number, he sat up. "Yo?" He answered. He quickly told Savannah to give him something to write with and a piece of paper. As soon as he had the information he hung up. He needed Savannah's help to accomplish his mission. But he knew that once he completed it that he would have to kill her. "Damn what a waste." He thought to himself as he stared at her naked body lying beside him. Might as well send her to meet her maker happy, Baby reasoned. He rolled over on top of her. Savannah stared into his eyes as she anticipated what he was going to do. He kissed her passionately on her mouth then lowered his face in between her legs. Savannah spread her legs as far as she could, giving him all access to her pearl tongue. As he licked and sucked on her with experience Savannah rolled her pelvis then began humping his face. She was close to orgasm when he stopped and entered her. His 9 inches felt like 100 to her as he slid into her slowly causing her to hold her breath. When she finally breathed, he was all the way inside of her. She wrapped her arms and legs around him and began kissing him wildly. Baby was amazed by her tightness and wetness but was even more amazed when he felt himself nearing ejaculation. "Damn I'm about to cum!" He tried to pull out, but Savannah was climaxing herself. Baby emptied his seed deep down inside of her after only three minutes.

After regaining his composure, he started laughing. "What's so funny?" She asked. "I ain't never came that fast before, I swear to God!" Savannah let out a cute laugh of her own. "Anybody ever told you that you look like..." she cut him off, "Don't say

Rihanna." "You get that a lot huh? Rihanna with a fat ass!" He

told her. "It's a shame I might have to kill this good ass pussy."

He thought to himself, as he just stared at her. "Why you

looking at me like that? So now you thinking I'm just another

freaky Atlanta girl huh? For your information you only the

second guy I've slept with." Savannah told him. "Come on now,

don't go there. You ain't gotta lie to me. I ain't judging you."

Baby assured her. "I put it on my mother's grave. Only reason I

came to your house was because my cousin asked me to come.

My boyfriend died almost a year ago, and I haven't been with

nobody since." She said with teary eyes. "How?" Baby asked.

"How what?" She replied. "How did he die?" Baby clarified.

"He used to rob people and robbed the wrong nigga. They

came back and they shot him in his head as we were coming out

of the club." Baby didn't know what to say. "I'm sorry for

insinuating you were a hoe, but if you were I wouldn't judge

you... I mean we all gotta do what we gotta do to survive." "I

don't have to do that, my brother looks out for me." Savannah

told him. "Oh you got a brother?" He asked. "Yeah, he

overseas right now, he was in the Navy." She said. "What he doing overseas?" Baby asked, trying to know as much as he could about her. Looking for a reason to not have to kill her. "He got kids in London and it's where his business is." She answered. "Business? What he do?" Baby asked. "He does contract work for the government. To be honest, I really don't know what he does for real." She answered. She went to the jacuzzi and filled it up with hot water. Baby rolled up a joint and when the jacuzzi was ready they got in together. The way he communicated with Savannah reminded him of Jazzy. Thinking of Jazzy made him reminisce about going to school with Low and LJ. Savannah was sitting in between his legs with her head leaning back against his chest. The weed helped remove his mind from the present and take it back in time. They were at Glenda's, Low's mother, house and Low had just came home from juvie. The look Low had on his face when he saw the candy apple red Camaro on gold 24 inch Dayton spoke rims was priceless. "I did that for my nigga!" Baby felt proud to be able to bless his nigga. All these years they had talked about coming up in the game and finally they had.

Baby was so withdrawn that he didn't even realize that Savannah had gotten up and was now sitting on the edge of the jacuzzi staring at him. The last memory that he had of his brother was the fight they had. All Low was trying to do was be his big brother and give him some game. Guilt filled his heart as the realization that his arrogance and ego had led to the death of his brother. "Damn I fucked up!" He closed his eyes, trying to catch the tears before they fell. Savannah didn't say a word she just sat there observing him. She had studied the mind of killers and what she saw in front of her intrigued her. Something was eating at his conscience and whatever it" was, it was something that he had done. When Baby opened his eyes, he saw Savannah sitting there staring at him. "What just happened?' He asked her. "You just zoned out. It's ok… I zone out too sometimes." She said, then rejoined him in the jacuzzi.

***

Wise pulled up to the club dressed to impress with all his ice on. Jennifer sat beside him looking like Ms. America. He sent

Godson, who was in the club already, along with his cousin from Long Island a text. His cousins were there to watch Godson's back, who was there to watch his back. $640k was a lot of money. Seconds later Godson texted him back. "Come on beautiful, time for us to make our grand appearance." Wise said to Jennifer. They got out of the black Cadillac Escalade rental and walked to the entrance of the club. "Yo, my name is Wise, Ed told me to tell you my name." He said to the doorman. "You good. Gon straight through." The beefy security guy at the door said. The people standing in line wondered who he was. Godson was sitting in a corner lowkey when Wise walked in and walked right past him. Diagonally across from where Godson was, Wise spotted his cousins. They were three deep. Wise went straight to the bar and told the chocolate bartender working who he was and she had a waitress come around and escort him and his white friend to a VIP booth. Seconds after they sat down in their booth Ed and his friend Soloman, who owned the shoe store that Wise had visited earlier that day, joined him. Ed was a big dude, 6'10" 270lbs, he was a giant. He put you in the mindframe of the guy in the movie life, starring Eddie Murphy and Martin Lawrence, who had the famous line, "you gon eat yo' cornbread?"

Soloman wasn't a basketball player, he was just a cool dude from the suburbs that he went to school with. Wise introduced Ed and Soloman to Jennifer. "I just need to know one thing Miss White Lady. How the hell did this fake ass New York con man get you?" Ed asked jokingly. Wise and Solomon fell out laughing. "We met at a West Virginia basketball game." Jennifer answered. "Got damn! I need to start going to college basketball games." Ed responded, causing Jennifer to blush. "Her father owns a real estate and development company." Wise added. Solomon gave him a high five. "A gorgeous, rich, white woman. We need to toast to that." Solomon said. Ed signaled for a waitress and told her to bring two bottles of champagne. "The good shit!" He added. "This is a nice place you got here Ed." Wise told his friend. "It could be better... I wanna get the upstairs as well and maybe put a nice stage in here and do karaoke night and live band nights... I want to draw a broader crowd." Ed said. "What's stopping you?" Wise asked. "It's expensive. I done already sunk $180,000 grand into this place. With the vision I have I'm gonna need at least another $150-200k to transform this place into something real special. Do some comedy nights for local comics to come for free and do their thing." Ed said. "$200k huh?" Wise looked around the club. $200k was a lot of money to a working man but it was peanuts to Wise. He had almost triple that amount on in the jewelry he was wearing. This might be just what he needed to clean his money. "So if I could get you the $200k would that be enough to make me a partner?" Wise asked. Ed thought he was joking, "Hell yeah it would." "How about next week?" Wise looked him in his eyes and said. Ed looked over at Solomon. Solomon looked at Wise. "I'm serious my nigga." Wise said, no longer smiling. "Let's make it happen then." Ed told him. "It's already done." Wise replied, then pulled out a cigar and broke it down. He rolled up a fat blunt of sour diesel. They sipped champagne and reminisced until Wise spotted Rasta walking through the club. "I see another friend excuse me." Wise said, leaving Jennifer with the wolves. Wise met Rasta at the bar. "Bredren me see you already start de parti witout mi you know." Rasta said with a big smile. "I ran into a couple guys I used to go to college with and we started reminiscing. But now that you here, we can talk business… big business." Wise said. "Talk to mi bredren. How big?" Rasta asked. "$640,000 big." Wise replied. "Now ya talking. Mi gwon do sum math and mi gwon put something nice togedda for you bredren." Rasta said as he signaled for the bartender.

"Mi wonna send mi friend an him compni tree bottles of ya best champagne ya preety gyal." The dark skinned bartender blushed. His accent was a aphrodisiac to a lot of women. "Mi also nee tree bottle of Remi Martan VSOP preety gal, tell me how much and Rastaman give it to you." Rasta had the bartender almost cumming on herself. He cashed out $2500 for the drinks, then gave the dark skin beauty a $500 tip. She slid him a napkin with her name and number on it. "Damn nigga, you on some Rico Suavè shit." Wise told him, as they walked to his booth trailed by two waitresses carrying their bottles, ice, and cups on trays. "Everybody this is a good friend of mine, Rasta. Rasta, this big country bumpkin is Ed, this is Solomon, and she... she's off limit's nigga. Rasta sat down and pulled a quarter pound of California OG kush out from under the front of his pants, then a plastic bag of natural leaf and rolled a gigantic blunt.

Chapter XVIII

Savannah just looked at Baby, as what he had just told her registered in her head. After a second round of steamy sex, they took a shower and got dressed. She knew something was up when she saw what he put on. The black baseball gloves were a dead giveaway, but she didn't speak on it. As they sat in the parking lot, a few parking spaces down from where Wise parked at The Gentlemen's Club, Baby told her the truth. "You can get out the car now and just walk away. I don't want to ruin your life, you got nothing to do with this." That wasn't what had her speechless. "You really were contemplating killing me?" She asked, still trying to wrap her mind around that. "It sounds evil but when you in the streets murder becomes something you learn to do to survive. It's not about bad or good, it's about survival and freedom. He robbed and killed my cousin. I can't go to the police, so I must be the one to see that he is held accountable for what he did." Baby explained to her. "Why not leave it in God's hands, he's the judge of all." Savannah reasoned. "Who is that?" Baby replied seriously, then lit the blunt in his hand. "You don't believe in God?" Savannah asked, while looking at him like he was an alien or something. "Not really, I mean if there is a God why so much fucked up shit be happening in the world? Where was God when Africans were being taken from their home and placed on boats? Where was he when white slave masters were killing us in front of our mothers, daughters, and sisters. Raping our women, treating us like animals… where God at right now in the hood? My people son just got killed on his 9th birthday! Where was God at?! Huh? My whole life God watched me go through hell." Baby found himself telling her his life story, leaving out nothing. It was a relief when he talked about Low, and that how he felt responsible for his death. "And what really hurts is I think it's one of my niggas who thought, at the time, they were avenging me." He confessed. Savannah had studied the criminal mind in school sure, but nothing in her college courses could give her this in-depth look into the mind of a young black man such as Baby. He had destroyed almost everything she thought she knew, at the least, he made her question it.

"Look, if something was to go wrong and something happens to me it's $50,000 dollars in the safe in the room. You can take it and pay your school tuition. If there is a God, maybe I can balance out all my wrongs." He said, handing her the hotel room key. Savannah knew she should have just gotten out the car and put as much distance between her and him as fast as she could, but she didn't. She felt sympathy for him. She was far from an angel herself, but she recognized the fact that there was a higher power above herself. "Baby you don't have to do this. Right now is when you need to believe in God and trust in his supreme wisdom. Everything happens for a reason. There is no such thing as chance or coincidence. Whatever happens was meant to happen. God gave us free will and with that free will he tests us. He's testing you now." Savannah tried to get through to him and for a second, she thought she succeeded. "You sound like a preacher girl." He said, with his charming smile.

How could a warm smile come from someone in so much pain

and confusion. "I'm the daughter of a preacher. My parents

were into church real heavy." She confessed. "You mentioned

that your mother was dead, so what's up with your father?"

Baby asked her. Savannah looked out the windshield as she

thought about the relationship between her and her father. "My

father wanted a life for me that I couldn't live. Like I said, I

believe in God, but some of the things I was taught as a little girl

doesn't make sense to me. Like a child born gay. How can it be

a sin if God allowed them to be born gay?" She queried. "I

don't think children are born gay. I read something one day and

it was talking about why homosexuality is on the rise these days.

The hormones they put in the meat and the cloning of our

produce is messing up the chemicals in our bodies, throwing our

systems all out of control. That's why little girls say they feel like

boys and vice versa. One thing I don't believe in is being gay.

But I don't judge em. How can I when I enjoy having sex with

two women??" He said with a smile. "I'm a hypocrite ain't I?

Listening to you talk I can tell you are very intelligent. You go from hood to intellectual like this!" She snapped her fingers. They had been sitting in the car for hours talking and smoking, until Baby got a text, and just like that he switched to kill mode. "When I get out the car, pull out of the lot and wait for me on the street okay?" Baby instructed. "Please Baby, you don't have to do this." Savannah's eyes began watering. Something told her that things were not going to go as he planned.

Wise was in the bathroom talking to Godson. He had just told him about the business deal that he had arranged with Ed for a 50% partnership in the club. "This is just the beginning son. I know you think me killing Ramon was foul but this a wicked game we in, and to get to the top you got to step on a few toes. It wasn't personal God, it was business." Wise reasoned. The liquor and weed had Wise feeling too good. He had just admitted to Godson that he killed Ramon. "I'm bout to fuck Jennifer lights out Son. You better get her sister up to yo room. We can switch on 'em, you know I don't love these hoes for that long." Wise said with laughter. Godson laughed along with him. "But seriously. I'm a try to talk her into letting us train her out.

She's so high right now she'll go for it, watch." Wise said. While

at the stall, Wise sent his cousin a text. "I'ma meet you at the

hotel son." Wise said as he washed his hands and examined his

self in the mirror. Godson let him leave out first. "Yo, I had a

great night. Wish I could stay but I can't. Got me a beautiful

white woman to sink this chocolate Mr. Goodbar into!" Wise

told his friends. "You need some help?!" Ed asked with a wide

grin. Wise ignored him and turned to Rasta. "In the morning

bredren." He said. "In de mawnin bredren." Rasta replied.

Wise looked up and saw Godson leaving the club. He looked

over to where his cousins were and saw that they had already

left. Rasta gave Wise some dap then walked to the bar so that he

could chat with the bartender. "We gon get together for lunch

and talk a little more about the club." Wise told Ed. "Call me

when you wake up." Ed told him. Wise said his goodbyes to

Solomon then grabbed Jennifer around the waist and guided

her towards the door. The club was still in full swing as he made

his way outside. As soon as the night air hit him his stomach

began to turn. He had drank too much champagne. "I feel like

I'm about to throw up." He told Jennifer, as he handed her the keys to the truck. Baby pulled his Cincinnati Reds Pro Model down low over his eyebrows and walked as if he was going into the club. When he walked past a tinted out Tahoe with New Jersey plates he couldn't see the three men sitting inside the SUV. "Aye, what's up with dude. He got a hammer on him." One of Wise's cousins said, peeping the extended magazine that hung out the front of Baby's hoodie. Wise saw the guy in the red Cincinnati Reds hat approaching him, but he thought nothing of it. Baby wanted to get up and close so that Wise could look into his eyes and know who was taking his life, and why. He had talked to Wise at his cousin's funeral, so he knew Wise knew who he was.

He was 10 feet away from him when someone yelled "God watch out!" Followed by warning shots being fired. A bullet nearly tore Baby's head off. He ducked and pulled out his .40 caliber and started dumping back. Cars began trying to drive out of the parking lot to escape the barrage of bullets that were flying blindly. Baby's heart was pounding. It seemed like 1000 shots came from behind him, then shots started coming from the opposite direction. That's when he realized that Wise was shooting at him. They had him in a crossfire. He snapped another clip in and took off running, firing wildly. Godson pulled up beside Wise. "Get in God, hurry up!" Wise took one last look at Jennifer laying on the ground bleeding. "Help me!" Jennifer said reaching out to him. "Come on God!!" Godson yelled. Wise jumped in the car, leaving Jennifer there to die alone. "Fuck Son, what's going on?" Godson asked nervously. "That Jamaican muthafucka set me up." Wise replied furiously as Godson sped out of the parking lot. "We gotta get up out of here God." Godson told him, while he repeatedly checked his mirrors. "Turn, turn, turn!" Wise stated, but Godson missed the turn. Wise saw his window rolling down and turned and looked out the back window, thinking whoever was shooting in the parking lot was behind them. "Yo son why..." Wise stopped mid-sentence. Godson pulled the trigger and blew his brains out the passenger side window. Godson stopped the car, opened the door, and pushed Wise's body out the car into the street and drove off. Police cars came from everywhere. In the midst of all the chaos the SUV with the New Jersey plates drove right past the cops. The driver of the Tahoe was in tears. He had to leave his brother's dead body in the parking lot of the club. Savannah sat and watched the entire ordeal unfold. It was the longest 3 minutes of her life. She waited exactly where Baby told her to wait, but once the shooting started he had to run away from her to stay out of the line of fire. By the time the shooting had stopped the police were pulling up. She couldn't understand how they got there so quickly. "Drop the gun!" The black officer yelled. Baby looked at all the Atlanta Police Officers with their guns turned on him and thought "this is it." "Baby please drop the gun!" He heard Savannah yell out of nowhere. He searched the crowd until he found her. He just stared into her eyes. "Last warning! Drop the fucking gun!" The police officer demanded. "Please don't kill him." Savannah yelled, as hot tears poured from her eyes. All Baby could think about was no more pain, no more disappointment, no more trying to please everybody…

Then he thought about the child Jazzy was carrying and his daughter Queen. He dropped the gun and got down on the ground. The police swarmed him. They saw the white woman lying there bleeding severely. They started beating him mercilessly. Savannah tried her best to help him but by the 3rd blow Baby was unconscious. "They gonna kill him!" Someone in the crowd yelled. None of the officers knew that he had recently suffered a traumatic brain injury. The paramedics arrived and went straight to Jennifer who was barely holding on to life. One of the black officers noticed that Baby was unresponsive and knew that they had went too far. "That's fucked up! They killed him." Someone in the crowd yelled. When Savannah heard that she dropped to her knees and sobbed. It was like reliving the night her boyfriend was murdered. She cried for the both of them. "Y'all ain't about to get away this time!" A young, black, male, who had been sitting in his car when the shooting started, said. Thanks to his smart phone he had the shooting and the beating recorded on his phone. he knew he could get some money for the footage he had. seeing how Savannah was sobbing he figured she was the girlfriend.

Chapter XIX

Channel 19; Fox News, Cincinnati Ohio

The Atlanta Police Department (APD) has arrested a local resident and charged him with murder, attempted murder, and four counts of felonious assault. Antwan "Baby" Johnson, according to homicide detective Gregory Washington, is tied to several murders and dozens of shootings in Cincinnati. China didn't hear anything else the newscaster said after hearing Baby's name. She was sitting in her living room after just getting home from work. She picked up her cell phone and called her Aunt Regina, then she called LJ. By that afternoon, Baby was the topic of Cincinnati. On almost every block they were talking about him. A lot of people didn't even know that he was out of his coma.

Fred was riding with Gudda talking to him about the time he had spent in Atlanta with Baby, LJ and Slime. "Bruh got a big ass house down there. We was down dat bitch foolin' on some real live boss shit. I wonder what da fuck happened?" Fred said

out loud but was really asking himself. "Shit just been jumping

off crazy my nigga. I don't know who to trust out dis bitch naw

mean?" Fred said. "Oh my nigga, you know I know what really

happened to Kelvin." Gudda said. He looked over at Fred and

saw in his eyes that as soon as he told him about Squirl, Fred

was going to kill him. "Talk to me my nigga." Fred said, taking

a long pull on a blunt. Gudda broke down what happened and

as he suspected Fred was seeing blood. "Drive over to Prospect

right quick." Fred said. Gudda knew that Prospect was where

Squirl was from. "Naw bruh... I can't let you do know reckless

shit." Gudda said, trying to protect Fred from himself. "My

nigga! Take me to Prospect. All jokes aside." Fred said getting

madder by the second. In the end Gudda knew he couldn't deny

him, so he drove over to Prospect in Avondale. Prospect was

once a legendary street, but the Feds sent many of the hustlers

from the block to jail. Squirl was one of the few original

Prospect boys that was still free, gettin' money. When Gudda

pulled up on Prospect, Fred jumped out before he could even

put the car in park.

Squirl was leaning up against his car talking to Mack and a few other guys from the hood. As soon as Squirl saw Fred he saw murder in his eyes. They both began reaching for their weapons, Squril being the quickest. Squirl let off two shots that hit Fred in the chest but instead of dropping to the ground Fred raised his gun and squeezed the trigger. The two of them were so close to each other that every bullet that was fired struck flesh. Everyone stood around watching in a state of shock as Fred and Squirl shot each other. When the gunshots finally ceased, they were both laying on the ground bleeding, fighting for their lives. Gudda jumped out of the car and ran over to where Fred was laying. "What da fuck bruh! Hold on man, hold on!" Fred had blood coming out from his mouth as he fought for air. Gudda carried him to his car, laying him on the back seat and took off to University Hospital, a few blocks away. Squirl's friends did the same thing.

***

LJ, Slime, Flip, and Scooter were all sitting in Ashly's living room sick. It was Scooter who filled them in on the reason why

Baby had stayed behind. "I knew we shouldn't have left!" Slime said. "Where Godson at then?" LJ asked. "He on his way back down here. And the Science nigga, I took care of. We gotta go back." Slime said. "Naw, we gotta sit tight. He gon reach out to us, we just gotta be patient." LJ said, trying to keep Slime calm. "We ain't got no access to the money or the dope. What we supposed to do?" Slime asked. LJ had to catch himself before he spazzed out on Slime. "Is that all you worried about my nigga?!" LJ said, looking him in his eyes. "Godson got the money that Wise took down there to cop with." Scooter said, getting both of their attention. "Where that nigga at?" Slime asked. "He should be on his way back here." Scooter answered him. "When the last time you talked to him?" He asked. "He called me this morning. He probably checked into a hotel to lay low or something." Scooter said. "Call him." Slime was about to say something else when his phone rang. Only people that had his number was his baby mama and his mother so he grabbed the phone off the table. Seeing that it was Ladona, he answered the call. "What's up baby?" Slime answered. "Boy Fred and Squirl just had a shootout, they both in the hospital." Ladona said. "How you know?" He asked, forgetting about her cousin living on Prospect.

"My cousin said she was sitting on the porch when Fred pulled up and got out the car with some nigga with a black Avalon. She said he just start bussin." Slime knew Gudda had the black Avalon. "Did they say why?" He asked. "Nope. Oh and I seen Bop fat ass at Annie's last night too." She told him. "Annie's?? Fuck you doing going to Annie's?" Slime asked with an attitude. "My sister asked me to go with her. So if yo sister asked you to fuck a nigga you gon do it?" Slime said. "Fuck you Slime. Like you ain't fuckin somebody wherever you at. Miss me with that corny shit nigga! You want Bop number or not?" She said, clearly over Slime's shit talking. "Text it to me." Slime said and hung up on her. A few seconds later she sent him Bop's number in a text. Slime called the number. "Who dis?" Bop answered on the third ring. "The donut man you fat mufucka!" Slime said laughing. "What up bitch?! Man so much shit been going down boy, I'm glad you ducked off somewhere. You hear about yo boy Baby?" Bop asked. Slime put him on speaker phone. "Yea my baby mama just told me. I ain't even know that nigga was out the hospital. I'm salty at bruh for not getting at me." Slime lied. "Oh yeah and you know they said Squirl the one who got Kelvin up outta here." Bop told him. "Swear?" Slime asked. "Yeaaa my nigga." Bop told him. He explained everything to him. How Squirl felt some type of way over Kelvin telling everybody that he was the police. "You know him and Fred just had a shootout. They supposed to both got hit." Slime told him. "You good tho my nigga? If you need me just let me know." Bop told him. "I'm straight for right now, but I'll let you know if I need you." Slime let him know. "Aight fool hold it down. You know I got shit to do. Love you my nigga." Bop said, ending the call. "Love you too big bruh." Slime said and hung up.

Chapter XX

Baby opened his eyes and all he saw was a bright light. "Damn! Am I in Heaven? I'm dead?" He asked himself. Slowly his vision began to focus and he realized he was in a hospital room. He tried to lift his arm and realized that he was handcuffed to the bed. The door to his room opened, and a black female nurse with the tightest scrubs he had ever saw a nurse wearing, entered his room. "Sheesh!" She had hips and ass for days. "They bout to be calling the police letting them know you woke. My niece said don't worry she ain't ran off on you. You been on the news every day in a row this week. One of the shooting victims died a few days ago." She was saying so much Baby was trying to figure out who she was and what she was talking about. "How long I been in here?" He asked. "A week," she answered. "They beat you up pretty bad." A knock came from the door and seconds later the door opened. A white man, that needed to do some crunches, and a frail, skinny, black man entered the room. They both were wearing cheap suits, Baby knew they were the police. "Mr. Johnson we're glad you can finally join us," the black detective said. "You're in some real deep shit! We got three dead bodies, a woman who's been in critical for a week fighting for her life, and she's white! You know how it goes… A young black kid from the hood killing a white woman in Georgia, you're looking at the death penalty! You wanna help yourself? You need to tell us what happened?!" Baby just looked at the officer like he was retarded. He stared at them, they stared at him. He stared at them, they stared at him. Then the detectives looked at the nurse. "Is he all there? I mean… Does he understand what I'm saying?" He asked. "Sir… I'm just a nurse. I can't speak to his full mental state, however, I do know that he suffered severe head trauma. You guys will have to wait until the doctor examines him fully to get the specifics. Baby continued to stare at the detectives with a spaced out look. The nurse wanted to laugh but she held her composure.

"Girl, he had the police mad as hell. He just stared at them with this vacant look in his eyes." Tori told her niece as they sat in her living room. "I need to go get his lawyer up there to see him before they take him out of there." Savannah said. Tori was Savannah's mother's, youngest sister. Out of all her mother's siblings, Tori had always been her favorite. "Who did you get him?" Tori asked, referring to the lawyer. "I got Debra Hargrove." Savannah answered. Tori gave her niece a hard look. "Debra Hargrove." Tori repeated, because she knew the young black female lawyer was good and very expensive. "Yeah, he left me with $50k so I took $40k of it to her and kept the rest to make sure he had money when he got to jail." Savannah said. "Savannah, where you meet this boy at?" Tori asked. She knew her niece had poor judgment when it came to picking boyfriends. Before Savannah could answer, her cell phone rang. "Hello?" She answered the unfamiliar number. "Hello, is this Savannah?" A female voice asked. "Yes, this is she." Savannah answered. "Good afternoon, Savannah, this is Debra Hargrove." "Hi Debra. I've been waiting on your call." Savannah said. "I'm here at the hospital with Antwan. He wants to speak to you." Savannah gave her aunt a big happy smile. "School girl." Baby called her. His voice brung tears to her eyes.

"Hello, you there?" Baby asked, noticing silence. "Yes, I'm here." She answered quietly. "You ain't crying are you?" "No." She answered, lying. He knew she was lying though. "Ok listen up, I need you to call my people for me… You still got that phone I left in the car?" Baby asked. "Yes. I got it in my purse right here." Savannah answered. "Debra gon come and see you as soon as she leaves here. She has a note for you. You still got the hotel room?" Baby said. "No, but I got everything you left in the room." Savannah said. "You got the keys I left?" He asked. "Yes, I got em." She replied. "Aight." Baby answered. He knew he had to get the money out of the safety deposit boxes before Stacy got any bright ideas. "You all I got right now. Please promise me I can trust you Schoolgirl." He asked. "You can trust me, I promise." Savannah vowed. "As soon as you and Debra link up, I need you to go take care of it asap! Don't wait, and make sure you buy four duffle bags." He instructed. "Okay. I got you. I promise, okay??" She told him. "Yo, I'm glad I didn't do what I said I was thinking about. You 100." Baby said, reminiscing. Savannah knew that he was referring to when he told her that he was thinking about killing her. "Me too." She said, smiling at his joke.

Baby laid in his hospital bed after Debra left to go meet up with Savannah. He was thinking about the money that he had stashed in Stacy's name. He prayed that Stacy didn't try to take the money and run.

***

Stacy sat outside of the bank contemplating her next move. She knew that Baby was behind Julius's death after learning the Mexicans got robbed for $15 million dollars. She had gotten the safety deposit boxes in her name for him but he had the keys. She got out of her car and walked towards the bank thinking about how she could help her father pay off his loans with the money. Her father would never have to entertain the thought of jumping back in the game again she reasoned.

***

Chihuahua Mexico; The Sanchez Estate

Azael Vargas knew the Garcia's were behind the recent attacks on his family. The beef that he thought was over had resurfaced. The reason why, was something he didn't have the answer to at the moment, but he was damn sure about to find out. Hugo Garcia was a man of his word, so for him to "ok" an attack on his family, something or someone had to have provoked him. He sat in his study inside his fortified fortress of a mansion surrounded by armed guards. He summoned his son Jesus. "Yes father." Jesus said, entering the study. "I need you to get word to Hugo and try to find out what was the cause of the attacks… War right now with the Garcia's is not good for us. If we can resolve this, we need to. I've worked too hard to clean our name." His father directed. "Yes father." Jesus Vargas replied. He left his father's study talking on his cell phone. His quiet operation that his father knew nothing about had blown up in his face. If his father learned about his independent drug ring he would kill him his self. Unlike his father, who was against the narco, lifestyle. Jesus was fascinated and honored to be a descendant of notorious Mexican narco traffickers.

The rap music that he listened to only added to his desire to become El Jeffe. His father had distanced himself from his Sanchez bloodline by changing their last name and walking away from the family business. Jesus was drawn to it like a moth to a flame. One thing was for sure and that was that Jesus could not allow his father to find out about his unsanctioned operation. "Get rid of everyone, clean house." Jesus said into his cell phone before ending the call. He made one more important call. "Uncle." He said when the call was answered. "Jesus I'm hearing some bad things." The man said. "That's why I'm calling. You don't have to worry about anything. My people are cleaning house as we speak, and my father doesn't know anything." Jesus said. "What about the Garcia's? You have reignited a fire that can potentially burn us all." His Uncle said. "I don't know why all of a sudden they attacked us, but I'm going to find out." Jesus told him. "You better Jesus. For the both of our sake." the call ended

Chapter XXI

Baby had faced a lot of things in his young life, but none of the things that he encountered in the past compared to what he was facing now. Being locked up hundreds of miles away from home made it even harder. For the past 30 days he had been locked up in the Metro Youth Detention Center in Dekalb County. One minute he was on top of the world then in the blink of an eye everything changed. The possibility of him spending the rest of his life in jail was a reality that he had come to accept. Stacy betraying him was something that he could not accept. She had run off with $5 million dollars. He had never told her what he put in the safety deposit boxes, he just used her name to get the boxes. If she thought she was just going to disappear and live happily ever after, she was sadly mistaken. Slime and LJ would hunt her to the end of the Earth if they had to. "Johnson." The musclebound Corrections Officer said while opening his cell door. "What?!" Baby asked, standing up from his bed.

"Your lawyer is here to see you." He said. When Baby got to the small room, that was designated for attorney visits, Debra Hargrove was there waiting for him. Debra looked more like a video vixen than a lawyer. Behind the hourglass shaped body and pretty face was a fearless and intelligent black woman from the hood. "Mr. Johnson." She said standing up outstretching her hand. The guard that had escorted Baby walked out of the room, leaving them alone to talk privately. "How you doing Baby?" She asked, addressing him by the name he preferred to be called. "Have you found anything out?" He asked. "I'm not a private investigator Baby. The people you hired are very good, give them some time. You don't need to worry about nobody but yourself right now. Now like I expected your case will be tried in the adult court system. You have a court date for next week, where a judge will bound your case over. Afterwards, you will be transferred to the county jail." Debra explained. "Then what?" Baby asked, with a nonchalant demeanor. "Then we start fighting. We're going to make them prove their case. We have a story, and they have a story. We have our evidence and they damn sure better have theirs. This is going to be a long fight so get ready to rumble." She said. Baby cracked a quick smile. He liked her attitude. "So I can count on you to fight for me?" Baby asked. "You can count on me to do what you pay me for." Debra countered. Since the first day she met him, Debra knew something was special about the kid. His persona was big. She understood immediately that he was used to playing by his own rules, doing things the way he wanted to do them. The judicial system meant nothing to him. He didn't believe in anything outside of his self and money. "So it's all about the money huh? As long as I keep the money coming in, you'll fight as hard as you can for me?" He asked. "I'll do everything in my power." She answered. He stared into her eyes as if he could read her mind. She actually liked his fearlessness, and he knew it. The fact that he worried more about the child his pregnant girlfriend was carrying, as well as his mother, let her know that he was a loyal and honorable person. "We need to talk about the money." She said, breaking the silence. "What is there to talk about?" He replied. "What's understand don't need to be explained. If I have to spend the rest of my life behind these walls that's a fate im willing to accept.

My children and my mother are the treasures of my life. I need to know you will do what you swore you would do." He finished. "I'm a woman of my word Baby. It's all in the contract I drew up." She told him. "Well… I guess I'll see you in court next week then, Ms. Hargrove." Baby said as the ended the meeting.

Chapter XXII

"You need to slow down on all that shit." LJ said. Slime looked up at him with cocaine residue all over his nose. "You need to try dis shit, it'll loosen yo tight ass up." Slime replied, as he offered him the tray of cocaine he was snorting from. The two naked females sitting on the couch beside him reached out for the plate simultaneously. "This nigga! Fuck he think he is?!" LJ mumbled as he walked to his bedroom. After unlocking his bedroom door, LJ walked to his closet where a four foot tall safe was. After turning the dial until he put the correct combination in, he opened the safe. He dumped the bookbag he was carrying, spilling blocks of neatly rubberbanded money onto the floor. His cell phone vibrated on his hip. A smile appeared on his face as he looked at the number calling him. He answered the call and listened while the electronic greeting directed him to press the number "0" to accept the call. "What's up John Gotti?" LJ said. "What's up Big Bruh. What's going on in your world?" Baby asked. "Same ol' shit, you know me, taking it slow like a turtle. But ya boy… Awe man, he done turned into Tony Montana." LJ told him. "What he doing yo?" Baby asked with laughter. "Snorting his brains out. Man, he downstairs right now sitting in the living room on some geekin' shit wit two coke head bitches." LJ said. "Take that nigga the phone." Baby told him. When LJ got to the living room, Slime had one of the girls in the doggy style position while the second female stood over the girl thrusting her pelvis into Slime's face. "I wish you could see this nigga right now." LJ said. "What he doing?" LJ explained to Baby in detail, painting a vivid picture for him to visualize. "Why you ain't trashing them hoes with him?" Baby asked. "I'm focused on business. Without me this shit a be all fucked up. Yo boy Flip on some Menace to Society O-Dog shit. He running around with Scooter and them two lil niggaz think they in a movie. I wish you was out here I need some help with these niggaz." LJ said really missing his boy. "I talked to Fred a couple days ago too." He continued. "Word?" Baby responded, "What's up with dat nigga?" "He good. He got a lawyer he said he gonna free Gudda and take the case." LJ replied.

"You talk to Vivica?" Baby asked.

"Yeah, I gave her your info. Oh you know Low brother out. They say he fuckin with Wayne." LJ told him. "You heard anything new about Dae Dae?" Baby asked.

"Naw… What they talking about with you doe?" LJ asked him.

"Shiiid, I'm bout to rumble with these bitches, I'm innocent." Baby said with humor, but serious at the same time. "I know you are. They was trying to kill you bruh." LJ said, knowing their call was being monitored. Slime was so tuned in to the two women he still hadn't noticed that LJ was behind him. LJ walked up and smacked him on his bare ass causing him to jump. "What type queer shit you on? You see a nigga handlin his bidness and you touching all on a nigga! You on some otha shit forreal my nigga! Smack dey ass fag ass nigga!" Slime said, furious. LJ couldn't stop laughing. "Why you wanna touch my ass and it's two fat asses right here? It's starting to come out you boa!" Slime continued.

"Come on Daddy… I was about to cum again." The female that was down on all fours, moaned from the floor. "Lil bruh on the phone nigga, he trying to holla at you." LJ said, then handed him the phone.

"What's up blood?" Slime said into the phone.

"What's up with you Bruh? LJ told me you out there on some Scarface shit." Baby said.

"Man bruh on some weird shit. Nigga just smacked me on my ass while I'm banging one of my hoes out. That's that white boy shit... niggas don't play like that. You know all white boys gay for real?" Slime said.

LJ started throwing a combination of punches at him. "If you slip I'm beating yo ass. Like chill nigga, you see I'm naked... Why you trying to play wit a nigga while he still on hard anyway?!" Slime was high as giraffe pussy.

"Man shut the fuck up, you the one gay." LJ protested.

"Yall out there foolin' and I'm in here surrounded by a bunch of niggaz I don't know." Baby tried to bring them back.

"Don't trip fool... Dem crackaz can't keep you. You gon beat dat shit then we gon go find that wild ass bitch Stacy." Slime said as he motioned for the two females to join him back on the couch. One positioned herself in his lap by straddling him the other one straddled his face. "Lil bruh, I got some expensive pussy in my face, listen to this right here. Make that shit clap for my lil brother Baby!" Baby listened to the sound of her ass clapping over Slime's face and started thinking about Jazzy.

He listened to Slime until the phone call ended.

He dialed Jazzy's number, expecting to hear the voicemail like he had been hearing, but this time it rang.

"Aye boy you know you ain't the only one got somebody to call!" Somebody said.

"Hello." Jazzy answered. Hearing Jazzy's voice instantly brought a smile to his face. So he ignored Roc, the pod bully. Since arriving at the facility he had watched Roc bully the entire block. For a 16-year-old, Roc was a giant, standing every bit of 6'4 and weighing close to 250lbs.

"I've been trying to call you. Is everything ok with the baby?" Baby asked Jazzy.

"Baby! I tried calling your phone a million times. What are you

doing in jail?" she asked, beginning to freak out. She was ready

to tell her Uncle to stop the car and cancel her visit with her

father.

"They got me locked up in Atlanta. They charged me with

double-homicide and a bunch of other shit." Baby told her.

"You think you the only killa in here nigga?!" Roc said,

menacingly for everyone, including Jazzy to hear.

"I'll holla at you when I get off the phone..." Baby told him,

looking him in his eyes. "Jazzy, LJ got a new number 513-929-

1039. Call him and he'll let you know what's going on." Baby

instructed her.

"Baby no! You can't go to jail. I need you." She began sobbing.

"Don't worry. Everything gon be okay. You know I always land

on my feet. I need you to come see me tho. I'm gonna call you

back. I gotta go, I love you." Baby said. "I love you too

Antwan." Jazzy said with tears in her eyes. Hearing those words

come from her recharged his spirit.

Before he could hang the receiver up Roc hung the phone up. The entire pod zeroed in. Roc's minions stepped up ice grilling him.

"I thought you was a super tough nigga, you need help?" Baby asked, returning the hard stares. He wasn't intimidated one bit. Fighting was something he grew up doing. Although he was hundreds of miles away from home and all by himself, there was no bitch in him whatsoever. He had a reputation to uphold.

"Yo Roc! Beat dat nigga ass!" One of the minions barked.

"He don't need no help, y'all fall back." A brown-skinned, stocky dude said, stepping up.

Baby looked at the quiet dude that stayed to himself, puzzled by his sudden speaking up on his behalf.

"You know dis nigga Jabril?" Roc asked, just as puzzled by his interjection into the situation as Baby was.

"Yall niggaz think everybody cock. You don't know buddy. He don't fuck with nobody, he was on the phone. All you had to do was say you had next. You been barking ever since you been here… time to bite nigga." The guy, Jabril, said.

"Man fuck him! He ain't even from 'Da A'," Roc snapped.

Baby cracked him, surprising everyone. The punch was loud and hard, but Roc ate it. There was no taking the punch back, so he kept swinging, connecting almost every punch. Roc wasn't going down for nothing in the world tho. Roc swung two wild hooks that Baby easily got under. "I can't let this big mufucka Grab me!" Was all Baby kept telling himself. Roc got tired of eating punches and rushed in like a bull. Once Baby felt Roc's hands on him he knew it was over. One minute he was on his feet, the next he was in the air coming down to the ground. All he could do was protect his head. The sound of his body connecting with the hard tiled floor was loud.

Roc landed a hard right hand that split him above his left eye. Baby scrambled to his feet as Roc tried to pound him out while he was still down. Baby got to his feet, dazed. Blood was spilling down his face, as the guards stormed into the block screaming for everyone to get down. By then Baby had shook off the punch he had taken. Roc made the mistake of turning to see the guards and Baby capitalized off of it. Roc never saw the punch coming. Baby stepped into the punch looking like a professional baseball pitcher on the mound. The guards stopped dead in their tracks as Roc's body collapsed to the floor. Several of the guys were happy to see Roc finally getting what he deserved. He had been a problem all the years he had been coming there. Baby looked around the pod stopping to lock eyes with a guy named Jabril. Jabril gave him a slight nod. Baby complied with the guards and was handcuffed and escorted from the pod. All he could think about was how long would it be before he would be able to use the phone again?

Jazzy sat nervously waiting for her father to enter the visiting room. She had learned a lot from her grandmother about the man she called father. After 20 minutes, her father finally made his grand appearance. Hugo Garcia was a medium build, nothing about him stood out. He looked like an average Mexican man, at least, until you looked into his eyes. Jazzy got to her feet smiling like a kid in the ice cream parlor. The first thing Hugo noticed about his daughter was her huge stomach and his anger began to build. "Poppa." Jazzy said, with watery eyes as she wrapped her arms around her father for the first time in her life. Hugo's anger quickly dissapated.

"What happened to your eye?" Debra asked her client with concern. "I talked to Jazzy. I need you to call her and relay a message." Baby said, ignoring her question. Debra rebutted. "Do you need to be placed in Protective Custody? I can arrange it… I know being from an entirely different state can..." Baby stopped her mid-sentence. "I don't need protective custody. You fight for me in that courtroom. I can handle myself in here. You think this something? You should see him…" Baby said and gave her a sinister smirk. When Baby walked into the courtroom the first person he saw was Savannah. He scanned the room, present was his Aunt Regina and her husband, China, his Aunt Stephanie, Marlyn, Aron, Jamaica, Peaches, Frankie, LJ, and lastly, he saw Jazzy. The courtroom was full of his supporters.

The only person missing was his mother. The bailiff escorted him to the table where Debra was seated. As he sat down, he looked across the room and saw the Cincinnati Homicide Detective and his black female partner. "What the fuck they doing down here?" he asked Debra. "They asked to be here." She replied. "Are we ready to proceed?" The old, white man judge asks the prosecutor. "Yes your honor." The prosecutor announced. "All Rise." The bailiff said and the entire room complied. "Your honor this is The State of Georgia versus Antwan "Baby" Johnson." The prosecutor began reading of the long list of charges. "We are not here to determine whether you are guilty or not guilty do you understand?" The judge looked at Baby and asked. "I don't understand why I'm here in the first place, somebody tried to kill me. I got caught up in the middle of a shootout." Baby fired at the judge. Debra had a quick conversation with him that only the two of them could hear. "Sorry Your Honor, you may proceed." Debra stated. "Well thank you Miss Hargrove," the judge said sarcastically. The next 20 minutes was all a blur. All that Baby understood at the end was that his case would be transferred to the Adult Criminal Court System. When it came time for him to be escorted from the courtroom everyone there to support him began shouting 'they love him'. Baby walked out of the courtroom feeling like he just might come out of this ordeal victorious.

Back at Metro, Jabril was waiting for him when he walked back into the pod.

"So what did they do?" He asked, once they were inside Baby's cell. "They bound me over, so I guess I'll be going to the county jail." Baby answered.

"You a soldier, you gon be aight. I got a couple niggaz over there. I already sent word to them you my people. So you good, dey over there smoking big weed, eating good and everything. When I get out I'll come get at you. I should be out in 72 days." Jabril said.

"Johnson! Pack it up!!" The guard yelled.

"It ain't over, trust me. We gon link up out there on the streets and get a whole lotta money my nigga. So be there when I walk up out dis bitch!" Baby said confidently.

"I'ma be there. All you gotta do is come through Edgewood or anywhere on the East Side and ask for Jabril." After dapping each other up, Baby began packing up his things.

***

Carrol Washington was sitting in her living room watching the 12 o' clock news, when they broke the story she had been trying to keep up with. After the story about Antwan "Baby" Johnson went off she picked up her cell phone.

***

"Im sorry Mell. I didn't plan for it to be this way." Frankie sobbed.

"You let my son get killed, then you go get pregnant by a 17-year-old?! You one foul bitch. You know the rules my nigga. It's cool. I ain't got life… this 12 years gonna fly." Mell said, furious but calm.

"I love you Mell, you know that. I fucked up." Frankie sobbed.

Mell wanted to go in on her, but he couldn't, for the sake of his money that only she knew about. First, he had to secure his stash then he would sever ties with her. He couldn't allow her to make him look like a fool.

***

Wayne was feeling untouchable after almost killing Dae Dae and running off with the $250k that Gudda paid for the ransoming of his sister. Now with money behind him and Dae Dae's brother's help, Wayne had put together a team of young and old robbery boys. They were terrorizing the inner city with associates in nearly every neighborhood. He was able to select even more victims. Either they paid him, or they got paid a visit.

Wayne was driving slow down Vine St., Downtown, in his brand new, cocaine white 645 BMW. Trailing him were two tinted out Chevy Suburbans, full of his goons. He made an abrupt stop on the corner of Vine and Green St.

"What's up? Why you stop right here?" Eli asked, looking for the cause of Wayne's sudden stop. Wayne continued staring out the window. "That's that bitch ass nigga Mama right there." Wayne said in an almost whisper. "Who Mama? Fuck you talking about man?" He asked. Wayne watched Laura standing next to a young hustler. He could tell she was running licks for him. "That's Baby's Mama." Wayne said. "What's up?" Eli asked, clutching his gun. The robberies, murders, and shootings, that they had gotten away with made Eli think they were above the law. He was ready to jump out the car and murder Laura in front of the whole block in broad daylight. "Nah... Not now. Just make sure you slide back down here and get that dope fiend bitch up through. That's for Lil Mike and Johnny." Wayne said. Lil Mike and Johnny were two of Wayne's young soldiers that died the day Baby shot up his porch in Avondale. He knew that Baby was behind the shooting. It was retaliation for him robbing Gudda. "I got her. I'm a get Spike to put it together." Eli told him. Wayne put the car back in drive and pulled away from the curb.

***

Hugo Garcia sat inside another inmate's cell talking on his cell phone. On the other end of the phone was Azael Vargas. They talked for almost 20 minutes before Hugo ended the call. He handed the phone off and returned to his cell where he sat alone in deep thought. Everything Azael said made sense to him. He knew that Azael was unaware of his son's quiet operation with Roberto Sanchez. Jesus Vargas was distributing cocaine and heroin from Atlanta. The same day that Julius was killed, Jesus's stash spot was robbed. Hugo easily filled in the missing pieces and what he came up with pointed to Antwan Johnson aka Baby. Information was power, which was why he made alliances with people who made a living from gathering information. When he finally exited his cell, his security was posted up on each side of his cell door. "My people are on it. 18 from Chicago is on its way to Ohio as we speak. They have all the information they need." Spider informed him. Hugo stopped walking and turned to face his Lieutenant. "Tell your brother no mistakes. I want it done as messy as possible. Have him stay in Ohio, we don't need him in Chicago anymore. Ohio is a new market for us." He said. "What about the situation in Atlanta?" He asked.

"I'm waiting for him to be transferred to the County Jail. He's at DeKalb County Jail now." Hugo informed him. "I'll send word tonight." Spider responded. "Put 5000 on the fight tonight." He

said. "Which fight?" Spider asked.

Chapter XXIII

"Hey Gorgeous." The driver of the Dodge Challenger said, as

he pulled alongside Laura. She was walking the late night

deserted street, alone. It was 2:30 in the morning. Laura knew

what the driver of the car wanted. She stopped and peered

inside the car. "Get in baby, I ain't gon bite you. I'm just trying

to have a good time." He said. Something about the man's smile

alarmed her, her gut told her not to get in the car. The driver of

the Challenger sensed her apprehension, "Look. I'll give you the

money up front, look." He pulled out several $100 bills. After

Laura saw all the money in the stranger's hand, her mind

instantly started calculating all the dope she could buy. Her

greed and her addiction made her go against the warning bells

going off in her head. She walked towards the passenger side of

the car. "Ay' Laura," a crackhead yelled as he walked out from

the entranceway of the apartment building. "What Rabbit?"

She answered, with annoyance in her voice. "Give me a ride up

the hill to Clifton." Rabbit didn't wait for her to answer him. He walked up to her as if she told him to come on. "Find your own ride I'm busy." Laura told him as she reached for the door handle. "Ay' Playa, give me a ride up the hill man." Rabbit asked the driver of the Challenger. Laura got in the car and told the driver to pull off. Rabbit stood there cursing her out as the Challenger disappeared into the night.

DeKalb County Jail was nothing like Metro. As soon as Baby stepped into the cellblock he smelled weed. A tall, brown skinned, cocky dude with long dreads and a mouth full of gold teeth pulled up on him. He introduced himself as Slim and said that he was Jabril's homie. "So, you the nigga who knocked Big Roc out? You the one killed them New York niggaz Downtown huh? Jabril is like my brother, he official. I be calling his sister and she be merging our calls. I'm a call her tomorrow. You smoke?" Slim asked. "Hell yeah! Just tell me how much it costs. I want however much you wanna sell." Baby said. His first night in the county jail he smoked until he passed out. The county jail was a little more serious than Metro. On his third day there he witnessed a Mexican kid get stabbed by two other Mexicans. The 8th floor was where the violent criminals were housed.

"Damn my nigga, dude fuck around and die. The Mexicans ain't never getting out after that." Baby said. "The one that got stabbed up was a rat. Either they stabbed him up or get hit up they damn selves. You see the tall, skinny Mexican with the Cartier glasses on?" Slim said. Yea, who is he?" Baby asked, curiously. "That's Gonzo. He the leader of all of 'em. A couple days ago his sister's boyfriend and his entire crew was killed. They had a lil Mexican restaurant up north." Slim said. As soon as Baby heard restaurant, his mind began replaying the images from the restaurant Julius put him on to rob. "They're half Mexican, half Black. The nigga is Black Caesar, he from East Atlanta. That's Gonzo's right hand. They locked up on a double homicide case, but it look like they gon beat da shit!" As Slim was talking, Black Caesar looked up and caught Baby staring at him. "Johnson! You have a visit." The CO yelled. "Looks like you got a visit." Slim told him. Baby rushed to his room and got his self together, already knowing that it was Jazzy who had come to see him. But... that wasn't the case.

"You surprised to see me?" Baby was trying to understand why she was there? It had been a long time since they had kicked it together. "I seen you all on the news, you changed numbers on me. You're only 17?! You lied to me. So, I guess you're not a music producer either?" She ranted. "Look Carrol, yes, I'm 17. No, I'm not a music producer. I'm sorry for lying to you. Why did you come all the way down here to see me?" He asked, upset that she had taken Jazzy's visit. He knew that Jazzy was going to be pissed. "Because of your son." Baby was confused. It took several seconds for what she said to register in his head. "What are you talking about Carrol? What son?" Baby asked. She went inside her purse where she had several baby pictures of their son, Antwan Garvey Washington. Baby just stared at the pictures, as she held them up to the glass. "That's mine?" He asked with delight and admiration. "His name is Antwan Garvey Washington." She told him. "Where you get Garvey from?" He asked. Carrol let out a childish giggle. "When I first found out I was pregnant I was sitting in the house and a special about Marcus Garvey came on." She said. "So, since you had a black man seed in you, you named your son after a great black leader?" Baby queried. "I want my son to be great and to defy the stereotypes and statics I know he will face." She told him. "Where is he? Can I see him?" He asked.

"I didn't know how you would react, so I left him at the hotel with my friend. You know I don't believe what they're saying about you on the news. If it wasn't for you I would still be trapped inside a dead marriage. You inspired me to dream again. I'm in the process of opening my own boutique in Mason with my friend and daughter." She said, as her eyes suddenly began to fog up. She was thinking about his future. Baby stared into her eyes, and it was as if he transferred his energy into her through his stare. "I'ma be ok. I've been fighting all my life. I came from the gutter, grew up sleeping on a mattress and box spring on the floor. My father was locked up and still is. My mother was a crackhead. It was just me! I'm a survivor, so don't think just because you see me behind this glass it's over for me.

Smile don't be looking all gloomy and shit." He said, trying to comfort her. As tears rolled from her eyes, Carrol tried her best to smile. How could this boy make her feel things her husband couldn't? "Do you need help with the lawyer? What do you need me to do?" She asked. "My lawyer is paid already but put her number in your phone, that way she can keep you updated on what's going on. Put my cousin China number in your phone too. Oh, and my Aunt Regina gon wanna meet you too, let them meet my son." He continued. By the time the visit ended Baby was walking on air. As soon as he returned to the cellblock he jumped on the phone and called Carrol. They talked for nearly an hour. "So who was it that came and seen you?" Slim asked, after he got off the phone. "You wouldn't believe me, so I'm just gonna wait until you see the pictures. I got a son doe. This shit crazy man! I can't let these crackaz do me like they did my father." Baby said out loud. Slim's father was serving double life in a Georgia State Prison, so he understood exactly where Baby was coming from. "You trying to blaze up?" Slim asked. "Am I?! Come on fam you already know I am." Baby said. As they made their way to Slim's cell, Gonzo called out Slim's name. When Slim looked in Gonzo's direction, Gonzo made a motion with his hand as if he was flicking a lighter. Slim nodded his head then proceeded to his cell. Slim knew Gonzo was also getting his hands on weed, tobacco, and other contraband inside the jail. "Roll up." Slim said, handing Baby a pack of rolling papers and a small baggie of potent marijuana.

"My sister just asked me about him." Gonzo said. "So you think it's him?" Black Caesar asked. "It gotta be." Gonzo answered. "Shit let's go holla at him then." Black Caesar said. "That's why I asked him if he had a light. Roll up some of that weed we gon smoke with 'em." Gonzo said. Black Caesar nodded then got up and walked to his cell.

"What do you mean he already had a visit?! He ain't had no muthafuckin visit because I'm standing right here." Jazzy said, spazzing on a female guard working the visiting area. "Ma'am I'm sorry but Antwan Johnson had a visit a little over an hour ago." The guard told her. "Who came to see him?" Jazzy demanded. "Ma'am I can't give you that information." She replied. But seeing how far along Jazzy was in her pregnancy, on top of the fact that her driver's license was from Ohio, she felt sorry for her. "Listen, just this one time I'm going to let you see him. I know you drove too far to be told he already had a visit." Jazzy went inside her purse and removed 2 $100 dollar bills. "Thank you, I appreciate it. She handed the girl the two bills. The female guard snatched the money up quickly and pocketed it. She couldn't wait to get off work and hit the bar with the crispy $200 in her pocket.........

"My name Gonzo and this my homie Caesar." Gonzo said. "Baby." Baby said with a nod. "Where you from my nigga?" Black Caesar asked. "Cincinnati." Baby answered. Black Caesar handed him a small blunt rolled up in a rello. Baby looked at Slim. "Damn yall got rellos?" Slim asked. "I got some more coming in tomorrow. I'll holla at you." Gonzo stated. Baby blazed up the miniature rello. "What that is?" Baby asked, as he inhaled and tasted bud. "Kush." Black Caesar answered. "This immature. This ain't grown man." Baby said. Everyone in the room looked at him. Slim started laughing causing Gonzo and Caesar to look at him with animosity. "Naw, he told me the same shit when I put a couple blunts of the shit I got in him."

Slim told them. 'It's cool for now but I'ma get some of the shit

we smoke up my way in… y'all a see what I'm talking about. I

smoke rapper weed." Baby boasted. The cell quickly smoked up

but no one really cared. If you didn't make the guards work,

they just left the inmates to themselves. "You the nigga they had

on the news for killing them New York niggaz? This Cincinnati

police said you the leader of a drug ring." Black Caesar blurted

out.

"Naw man I ain't what they say I am. I'm just a regular nigga

trying to get some money." Baby countered. "Johnson! Visit!"

The guard yelled out. Baby looked at Slim. "It's another

Johnson in here?" He asked. "I don't think so." Slim said, as he

got up to look out the cell into the pod. Baby got up and walked

out of the cell high as hell. He thought he was tripping so he

went to the intercom and asked the CO. "You got a visit

Johnson." The guard told him. When he got to the visiting

room, he saw Jazzy. From the look on her face he knew that she

was pissed. "How did she get to visit him?" Was all he could think of. "Hello baby, how you feeling?' He asked. "Who da fuck you got coming to see you and you knew I was coming? You got me out here going against my father. He coming at me like he knows something I don't. Baby please tell me you ain't have nothing to do with what happened to my brother?" Jazzy ranted. "I swear on the child in your stomach that I had nothing to do with Julius getting killed! Believe me Jazzy. I didn't play any part in your brother's death." He told her as he looked into her eyes. "Who came to see you Baby?" She asked again. He figured there wasn't any sense in lying to her. He had to tell her sooner or later so why not now. "A female I used to mess with came all the way down here to tell me her son was mine. Me and her ain't messed around in like a year. The boy three months old. Me and you wasn't even together during that time so don't be mad. I want my son to know his brother, so I need you to meet her. And she older..." Baby told her. "How much older?" Jazzy asked. "She in her mid-30s… and she white." Baby confessed. "Ugh! You fuckin' old ass white ladies Baby?! Is she a dope fiend?" Jazzy said through clenched teeth. "Stop playing with me man. What the fuck I look like?" Baby shot back. "Nigga yo first baby mama was a dope fiend, so don't act like you don't be fucking dope fiends. You just trifling!" She spat. "Shut da fuck up and calm down. You know I was on some playhead shit before we got serious. So don't act like you surprised. Shit I'm surprised ain't nobody else done popped up on me." He said. "Because you a whore." Jazzy said. "And you're Mother Theresa huh?" He said sarcastically. That did it. She stood up and went off on him speaking in Spanish, not even realizing he couldn't understand a thing that she was saying. "You gonna come all the way down here just to argue with me Jazzy?" Baby said. She continued flipping out. He hung the phone up and got up. Jazzy didn't think he would really walk off, but he did, and she started sobbing.

Chapter XIV

"Wake up nigga." Baby opened his eyes to see Slim standing over him smiling. "What's up?" He said. In the the two weeks he had been in the county jail he had spent every day with Slim getting high. Once Jabril verified Slim was official, via a merged phone call, Baby lowered his wing to him. "Yo peoples met up with mine last night. Dis shit right here smell like 1000 pounds boy. Soon as I took it out the vacuum seal it had the whole pod looking around." Slim said. Bob must be in Atlanta Baby thought. He got out of bed and grabbed his toothbrush and toothpaste. As he stood over the sink, he stared at the pictures of his son hanging on a mirror. It was amazing to him how he created a smaller version of his self. "Roll up." Baby said. After brushing his teeth, he made himself a cup of coffee, a habit that he had picked up from Slim. Sitting on the edge of his cot, Baby thought about the conversation that he had with his aunt last night. She had fallen in love with his son already. Was he going to follow in his father's footsteps or be there to raise his son?

Growing up without a father was rough. He never got to experience going to a sports game with his Pops or tossing a football with him. He wanted to experience that with his son. "What's up man, you cool?" Slim asked, seeing that something was on his mind. "I gotta get out of here man, I can't go out like this my nigga. These muthafuckaz can't give me the death penalty!" Baby said. "It's one of them days huh? I know what you mean my nigga." Slim said. He was fighting an attempted murder charge and had been in the county for almost two years. All the weed did was keep him calm. When he wasn't high he was a totally different dude. A side that many feared. "Some days my nigga I wish I could rewind time. I think about if I wasn't born in the hood that maybe I would've turned out different. All this shit we do is because that's all we know... because it's what we grew up seeing. It's kill or be killed out there. Both my parents dope fiends. I've been out there since I was nine years old. I been lost my conscious." Slim said, as he stared off into space. It was as if he was recalling the exact day he had lost his innocence. After almost a full minute he snapped back and blazed up the joint that he had rolled.

As soon as he inhaled the potent marijuana he started coughing violently. He passed the joint to Baby, and Baby inhaled with no problems. "See... this real weed. Go get Gonzo and Caesar." Baby said.

"They must have moved him in last night." Gonzo said, referring to the new Mexican in the pod. "Damn! You smell dat?" Black Caesar asked, as the weed smoke drifted from Baby's cell into the pod. Gonzo got up from the table, leaving his breakfast behind. Black Caesar followed suit. The entire cellblock was lit up. The potent aroma of the Kush sent the block into a frenzy. Gonzo tapped on the cell door then peeked in. Slim waved him inside. Gonzo slid into the cell, followed by black Caesar. "Fuck is dat?" Black Caesar asked, upon entering the cell. "This that real shit I was telling yall about boa." Baby answered. "We should've got in the shower with this dis. Dis shit loud as fuck." Slim announced. Baby passed the blunt to Gonzo, who greedily accepted. Along with the two ounces of Grade A Cali Kush, Bob sent them flavored blunt wraps for them to roll up in. "It's a thick ass bitch working too." Black Caesar informed Slim. "That's Miss Williams. She normally work visiting." Slim, who had been there the longest, replied as he rolled another blunt. A tap came from the door and they all looked up. When Baby saw that it was Knowledge, a 5% that he had a few conversations with, he waved him in. "Peace God." Knowledge said as he entered the cell. "Yo God, my apologies for intruding, but I had to come see if I could bag a joint or two? I got commissary down there and money on my books, so I can pick you up some stuff when we go back to the store." Knowledge asked. "It's cool God." Baby said. He liked Knowledge. Every time they talked Knowledge laid some deep stuff on him. His entire life he never believed in a God in the sky. Knowledge opened his mind to a whole new way of thinking. The black man is God, Knowledge told him. Slowly, the entire block made their way to Baby's cell. A lot of them were Slim's blood homies. The 8th floor in DeKalb County is where they house serious offenders. Almost the entire block was fighting murder cases. Baby wasn't tripping over the weed but Slim charged everyone, even his homies. "Gonzales, Johnson, Hernandez... visits!" The female guard shouted over the intercom. "I can't move." Black Caesar said, causing everyone in this room to explode in laughter. When Baby got to the visiting room he saw Bop, his girlfriend Sharee, and Savannah waiting for him.

He couldn't help but notice the females who were there to visit Gonzo. Three of them in total and they were all dimes. Even Bop had to take several looks. Bop grabbed the phone first, "What up fool you good in there? Them Atlanta niggaz ain't trying to get none of that Dominican cookie is they?" Bop joked. "Shut yo faggot ass up nigga." Baby said laughing. From the jewels Bop had on, Baby could see he was doing well. "Man I wish you was out here lil bruh. It's going down that 80 way nah mean?" Bop said, confirming what Baby was thinking. "Hold me down... I'm on my way. You been checking on Gudda?" Baby said. "He called me this morning. You know he bout to get out on bond, but he gon be on the box." Bop answered. "What up with Fred, he getting out too?" Baby inquired. "Yeah, he gon get out. Me and LJ gon take care of everything. Carrol came to see me too. Mann that little nigga look just like yo goofy, cool looking ass." Bop said with a big grin. Share snatched the receiver.

"Boy yo son cute as hell! I hope he don't be no damn slut like his daddy!" "What up sis?" Baby said laughing. "How you holding up in there? I see you high as hell." Sharee said, noticing his eyes. "You trippin' sis!" Baby said. Bop snatched the phone from her. "You always doing something goofy! Turn yo goofy down." Bop told her, which resulted in Sharee spazzing out. Bop handed the phone to Savannah. "What's up big head?" Baby asked with a smile. "I'm good. How you doing? You got them books yet?" Savannah asked. Baby shook his head no. "I sent them three days ago so you should be getting them soon." She said. "I wanna tell you something." Savannah said. Out of all the females he dealt with, the relationship he had with Savannah was the calmest. He talked to her about everything. She knew about Jazzy and Carrol. "What's up Schoolgirl, don't tell me you scared to talk to me now?" Baby said. Savannah just stared into his eyes as she thought about what she had to tell him. Baby began to think about the money he had her holding down at the stash house he had in Smyrna. "You got me nervous. What's going on? Ain't nothing happen at the spot did it?" He asked, nervously. When he saw her smile he relaxed. "All that stuff is cool, but I'm pregnant." She answered. "What?? You bullshitting. Swear?" He asked. "I'm 7 1/2 weeks. I've been so focused on school and taking care of stuff for you that I ain't even realize that I ain't came on my period. This shit crazy." She said. Baby just chuckled to himself. "What's so funny boy?" Savannah asked.

"I'm thinking how many other females I got pregnant out there? I'm at 4 kids and I ain't even 18 yet." He admitted. "You need to slow your ass down. What's that one shit called when a man lives in one house with hella wives." She said. "It's called polygamy." Baby answered. "Yea that and nigga ain't nobody going for that shit. Yo white baby mama might, but ain't no black woman going for none of that shit so get that out your head right now." Savannah said. "So you mean to tell me if I bought a big ass mansion like the Playboy mansion you wouldn't live with me?" Baby asked. "You sound crazy as hell nigga. You need to sign up for medicine or something because you insane."

Savannah said laughing. "Stand up. Let me see that body."

Baby told her. When she stood up he reminisced on the sex they

had just before he had her drive him to the club the night he

caught his case. "Damn girl! Mmm mmm mmm. I hope our

baby don't fuck up that frame and turn you into a whale." Baby

said joking. Savannah gave him the middle finger. Bop had

made Sharee so mad she left the visit. Now Bop was talking to

one of the females that was visiting Gonzo. "Your brother a

dog, I should tell on his ass." Savannah told Baby as she

watched Bop get the girl's phone number. "Mind yo business.

What Sis don't know, won't hurt her." Baby warned her. "I

don't like him no more." Gonzo was speaking with his sister in

Spanish. "It's him. Word is, he killed Julius after they robbed

Fernando." Gonzo's sister stated. "I keep thinking someone is

going to come for me and Theresa. Gonzo, I'm scared." The

female said. "Ain't nobody gonna do nothing to you. I got the

homies on go. You just continue doing what you doing. Hector

gon drop the rest of that money off to you tomorrow." Gonzo

said. "They might work a deal if you turn him over Gonzo. All

they want is him. Fernando said 10 million in cash and 300

things were taken. That's a lot Gonzo. They'll kill me, Theresa, and Mama for that." She warned him. His sister had a valid point. "Keep this between us. Don't tell nobody Vanessa." Gonzo said. "I won't, but you just think about what I said Gonzo." She said. "I will, I love you." Gonzo said. "I love you too." He said.

"We gon take some pictures for you tonight, let you see the Benz I just pulled out. Oh yeah, and yo boy Red gave me a number for you. Call me and I'm a have it for you." Bop said. "Aiight bruh, love you fool." Baby said. "Love you too. Here wanna talk to yo Baby Mama #4?" Bop said laughing. Savannah took the phone from Bop and mugged him. "You going out with them tonight? Make sure you get real fly for me and flick it up. You know you ain't got to worry about nothing now for real. And you might as well call my aunt and my cousin China to let them know you pregnant. Welcome to my cult, my child." Baby told her, laughing. "You need help boy. I love you, call me and let me know when you want me to come back down here and see you." She said. "Smack dat ass for me before you leave." Baby said. "Yeah right, bye stupid." She said, blowing him a kiss before walking away. Baby stood there purposely, until Gonzo and Black Caesar's visitors left. He checked out the beautiful Mexican females, locking eyes with one of them. "Man she was strapped, who was that?" Black Caesar asked Baby, when they returned to the pod. "That's one of my chosen few. She just told me she was pregnant. That's gonna be baby number 4 for me." Baby said proudly. "Damn boy. Child Support gon kill you." Caesar said. "Naw I takes care of mine, they ain't gonna even need to go that route. I get money for real. I don't know what y'all be doing but me and my niggaz get it in, that 80 way." Baby told him. "What is that 80 way?" Gonzo asked. They were in Black Caesar's cell, getting ready to have another smoke fest. "It's just something we say. Like how they used to do it back in the 80's." Baby explained. After smoking three nice sized blunts Baby went to his cell. He was reading a book Knowledge had given him, called Nation of Gods and Earths, when Slim came and knocked on his door. "What's up fool?" Slim said, pulling the door up. Slim went inside his jail issued pants and pulled out a Philly steak and cheese sandwich. "I know you want some of this." He said.

"Hell yeah." Baby responded. "Aye Ms. Williams on yo dick boy." Slim said. "Why you say that?" Baby asked. "Nigga she gave me this sandwich and told me to bring it to you." Slim said as he broke the sandwich in half. They quickly devoured it. "I'm bout to hit the shower then make a few phone calls. What's up with that tobacco? See if you can get a couple squally's for me." Baby said. "I'll see what I can do." Slim told him, then walked out the cell. Baby grabbed his things for the shower and left the cell also.

When he walked out of his cell he saw the white guy whose cell was next to his, talking to a Mexican on the range. He overheard his next door neighbor say, "real cigarettes?" and he stopped and walked back. "Y'all got squally's for sale?" Baby asked. "I don't, but he does." The white guy said, pointing to the dingy looking Mexican. "When I get out the shower I'm a holla at you." Baby said. The Mexican just nodded at him.

As he washed himself, he thought about his baby mamas and the children they were carrying. The book he was reading was talking about how the black man was the Sun, and as the Sun shines it lights on the earth, it brings forth life. The black man

shines his light, which was knowledge, wisdom, and

understanding, onto the black woman who in turn, reflects that

light to the child. He was intrigued by the theology of the book.

It sparked an interest in him to learn more about his self and

creation as a whole. The black man's true nature was

righteousness. Only a righteous black man was a God. To be a

God, one must carry himself in such a manner. Which meant he

must act in accordance with his beliefs, which was righteousness.

In order to be righteous, you must think righteous. Baby

contemplated over what he had read as the hot water relaxed

his mind. He had never been religious, growing up no one had

ever explained to him who God was. In turn, he never really got

into the religion thing. His religion was getting money and

flexing. Seeing himself as a God with the ability to manifest his

thoughts into reality made him view life differently. He finished

washing up and walked back to his cell. He saw his neighbor still

talking to the Mexican with the cigarettes when he walked past.

He walked in his cell and began getting himself together. He

was putting on his shirt when the steel door opened, his back was to the door, so he turned to see who it was that was walking in his cell. Before he could turn completely around, a sharp pain soared through his back. All type of alarms started going off in his head. Fear began to grip him as the realization of someone was stabbing him hit him. He turned to see the Mexican, who was just talking to his neighbor, swinging a knife at his face. He felt the knife sink into his face and hit his bone. Adrenaline pumped heavily through his veins, as fear disappeared, and anger flooded his conscious. "You trying to kill a God?!" He shouted at the Mexican.

The Mexican was stunned by his sudden burst of energy. Baby faked a right hook and shot a blind uppercut with his left that wobbled his attacker. Baby grabbed his wrist, trying to knock the knife loose from his hand. The Mexican looked weak, but he was actually very strong, feeling his strength leaving him as blood pumped from the wounds he had sustained, Baby did the only thing he could do. He bit the Mexican's face. The Mexican let out an eardrum shattering scream and dropped the knife. Baby picked up the knife, as his cell door was yanked open. He began plunging the knife into the Mexican over and over until Slim shouted his name. Slim just stood there speechless, the cell looked like a slaughterhouse, blood was everywhere. Slim wasn't a hoe ass nigga but looking at Baby covered in blood and holding the bloody knife, he stepped back. Baby grabbed the Mexican by his hair and drug him onto the range. The entire pod thought what the hell was he doing, and just looked up at him. Baby locked eyes with Gonzo. "You think you can kill a God?! Come On!!" He released his hold on the Mexican's hair and began walking towards the stairs. "Slim what's up with yo boy man?" Gonzo asked nervously. By the time Baby reached the bottom of the stairs his vision began to go dark. He began swinging the knife wildly until he collapsed to the floor. Kimberly Williams rushed into the cellblock and saw Baby laying in a pool of blood. She had only been working at the county jail for 10 months. "Call for help!" Slim screamed at her.

Chapter XXVI

Frankie stared at the TV in a daze. She was in disbelief at what she was watching. A mugshot of Laura was on the TV screen. Her body was found that evening at Winton Woods, the news reporter said. Frankie thought about the last time she saw Laura on the visit to the Justice Center. Before she could pick up her cell phone to call China, China was already calling her. "Hello." Frankie answered. "Frankie! My aunt just called me and told me Baby got stabbed up real bad!" Frankie covered her mouth with her hand, since learning she was pregnant, she had been avoiding her friend. She had never told China that she slept with Baby that weekend that they went to see him in Atlanta. "I was just watching the news China and they had his mother on there. They found her body in Winton Woods." Frankie said

through sobs. "Are you serious?! Oh my God, I need to call my

aunt." China said.

***

Debra Hargrove was awakened out of her sleep with a call

informing her that one of her clients had been rushed to Grady

Trauma Unit. Debra jumped out of bed and dressed quickly in

a pair of blue jeans and gym shoes. As she drove to the hospital,

she called a friend of hers who worked at the county jail. By the

time she arrived at the hospital she had somewhat of an

understanding on what had transpired. While she waited for a

doctor to tell her the specifics of Baby's injuries, she called

Savannah. When the doctor finally approached her with the

news, she was relieved to hear that none of his injuries were life

threatening. The doctor said that most of the damage had been

done to his face. No visitors were allowed to see him. Once she

knew that he was okay, Debra began trying to gather as much

information as she could. Tomorrow she would make a call to a friend that she knew would know something.

"Come on Jeff, I know you at least heard something worth telling me." Debra pleaded. "You think you can just call me and I'll come running ready to do anything you ask huh? You haven't called me in nine months. I still don't know why you left me!" The man countered. "Oh my God Jeff, it's been almost a year. I left because I wasn't ready to put my career second, what you wanted I couldn't give you. That's why I left. You're a great man and the sex was almost fantastic, but you wanted a housewife, and I don't want that for my life right now." Debra told him. "So, are you seeing someone else now?" He asked. "No. I haven't been with any man since we split." She told him. "I miss you Debra. My life hasn't been the same since you left." He said with sadness in his eyes. Debra placed her hand on top of his and looked into his eyes. "Jeff. What you need I can't give you, all I can give you is sex. I don't want to be a housewife. I was with the same man from 17 years old until 28. You helped

me get over that. I don't have time in my life right now, I'm

enjoying my freedom and my career. A friend is all I want right

now." She told him. Jeff Gray worked for the Atlanta Police

Department, DeKalb County. His older brother, Jason, worked

for the DEA. During their four year relationship, the Gray's

treated her like family. Jeff's mother still called her to this day.

"All I know, as of now, is that the 21 year old Mexican never

should have been in the same cellblock as your client. Also, the

knife that was used wasn't your typical jailhouse Shank. It was a

5 inch stainless steel survival knife. How it got inside the jail, I

don't know. Debra's thoughts drifted to her 17 year old client.

She needed to have a talk with him. The Mexican had been

placed in that cellblock on purpose. It was a hit. Someone with

influence and connections wanted Antwan "Baby" Johnson

dead, and she needed to know why. "It was good seeing you,

Jeff." She stood up from where she had been sitting. They were

at a popular café on Peachtree, in Downtown, Atlanta. "Wait…

Debra." He said. "Can I see you this week?" Debra gazed into

his hazel eyes. Jeff was fine as hell, she couldn't deny that. He was tall, broad shouldered and very well endowed, the man was downright blessed. But the truth was, she didn't love Jeff. She had love for him, but she wasn't in love with him. She could use a good stroke from a man though, she thought. The past nine months she had been using her toys. "We can get together." She said, with a mischievous smirk. Jeff gave her a kiss on the cheek and watched her walk out of the café.

For three days Baby lay in the hospital, floating off the pain medicine they were giving him. Just so happened that Savannah's aunt, Tori, was his nurse again. "Aye, I need some of them pills to take back to the county with me. I got you Auntie." Baby asked. "Boy, you ain't about to get me fired and locked up in a cell next to you." Tori admonished him. "They ain't gon find 'em. And I'm gon pay whatever you charge me. What you want a purse or something?" Baby said with a smirk.

***

"That's my word Slim. I don't know what that shit was. We both from Atlanta so I do know this. Baby was fucking with ol' boy

Julius. He had a little car lot out in Smyrna. You know that shit that happened to my sister boyfriend right?" Slim just nodded his head. After Baby got taken to the hospital a riot almost jumped off in the cellblock. They locked the block down for three days while they investigated the stabbing and murder. The tension was heavy on the block between the Blacks and the Mexicans. Some of the Black's suspected that Gonzo was involved. Gonzo continued, "Word is, Julius set the lick up for Baby and his friends to hit. They took like 20 million in cash and dope, then killed Julius to cover their tracks. The New York dudes must have been in on the lick or he cut them out. Whatever it is, Baby got a lot of people that want him dead. You see what happened to my sister's boyfriend and his entire crew?? And they were straight up gangstaz. Whoever they were working for sent that guy in here to kill Baby. You seen that knife? That wasn't a Shank, that was a real knife! I'm gonna let you talk to my sister, I ain't lying to you bruh. I'm telling you the honest to God truth." Gonzo pleaded. Slim got up from the metal stool that was connected to the table and walked away to where a group of Blacks were waiting, ready to set it off if Slim

gave the word. "What's good blood?" One of the inmates
inquired, as Slim rejoined them. "Stand down for now." Slim
said, addressing the entire group. He walked upstairs to his cell.
"Peace God." Knowledge said, tapping on Slim's cell door
seconds after Slim stepped into his cell. "Can I come in?" He
asked. Slim waved him in. "What's up Knowledge?" Slim asked.
"I wanted to pull your coat to something." Slim stopped and
gave him his full attention.

"The night they brung that Mexican to the pod, it was like one
in the morning. CO Martinez brung him through. Before he
locked him in his cell, they stood there talking for almost 15
minutes. He kept showing him something on a piece of paper."
Knowledge told him. Slim stood there processing what
Knowledge had just told him. In the back of his mind, he heard
God telling him what he heard. Maybe there was some truth to
what Gonzo said. He smoked a joint with Knowledge then went
and got on the phone. "Yeah, this shit wild my nigga." Slim said
into the phone. "I don't give a fuck about no Mexicans! Lil
buddy a real nigga, I fucks with him. Keep that Gonzo nigga

close, rock his ass to sleep. Yo and I had spoke to lil buddy cousin, she said he was okay so they gon be bringing him back in there in a few days." Jabril said. "I got you boy. That's on blood!" Slim vowed.

Meanwhile at Grady Memorial Hospital, Debra was sitting with her client trying to talk some sense into him. "I ain't going into no protective custody, fuck I look like? My name is Antwan Muthafuckin Johnson! Fuck them Mexicans!" Debra had just informed him of his mother's death. From that point on he went on a tirade about how he was going to "murder all the fuckin Mexicans". "You need to tell me what's going on Antwan. I can't help you if I don't know what's going on." Debra tried to reason with him. His gown had come open, exposing his torso. His stomach and chest were scarred up pretty bad. She couldn't help but to stare. "You're going to have to tell me something or I'm removing myself from your case and the $1,000,000 that you have me holding, in which I can lose my license over, I'll turn over to the FBI. I'm not going to be risking my career and freedom for someone who's not telling me everything. Now what the hell is going on?!" Baby closed his eyes, and for the first time in a long time he just started sobbing. He was crushed over the death of his mother, knowing that she died because of him made the pain even deeper. Debra did the only thing she knew to do in the moment, and that was comfort him in his time of need. She held his head on her bosom while rubbing his back. His moment of weakness was short lived. He regained his composure and he made her swear that what he was about to tell her she would never repeat to anyone.

"I'm a gangsta." He told her, straight like that. Then he painted for her a very vivid picture of his life. The things that he told her put goosebumps up her arms and at the same time fascinated her. To her, it was like reading one of the urban novel books that she loved to read. Her favorite Author was, Kwame. And her favorite book by him was "Dutch". Antwan reminded her of a young Dutch. "I told you everything Debra. I need to be able to trust you. Please tell me I can trust you. Because if I can't... He didn't finish his sentence, he just stared into her eyes. What she saw in his eyes frightened her. Debra had always flirted with danger. She had always been attracted to thugs, which was why she couldn't love Jeff. "You can trust me, I promise." She answered, but Baby knew he had her before she opened her mouth. Once he started crying her first reaction was to help him and right now he needed all the help he could get. He knew who was responsible for his mother's death, as well as his close encounter with death. Laura wasn't the best mother, but she was his mother. Therefore, someone was going to answer for what they did to her. The next morning, he was returned to the county jail… to the same cellblock.

***

"You tried to kill him Popa! He's the father of my child! If you kill him, you'll never have your daughter… I promise!" Jazzy screamed hysterically. Hugo wanted to tell her that it wasn't him who tried to kill Antwan, but he would be lying. "He can keep his life if you return to Mexico. But if you attempt to visit or communicate with him in any way he will die." Hugo said, matter of factly. Jazzy couldn't hold back the tears. Once she had learned of Baby's mother's death, she just knew her father was responsible. Jazzy knew Baby like no other and she knew that somehow, he would find her and their son if she did what her father said and returned to Mexico. As long as he had breath in his body, he would look for them. It was up to her now to keep that breath in his body.

To be continued…

"END"

Made in the USA
Columbia, SC
07 August 2023

21190937R00152